Jake stroked her hair. "I'm so sorry. I know Quinn was everything to you, as you were to him. He was so proud of the woman you'd become. You couldn't have made him any happier."

She raised her head from the shirt she'd stained with her tears and took in the small house with a watery gaze. "Nothing will ever be the same again."

"Nothing ever is."

She balled her fist against her stomach. "What am I going to do?"

"What are you going to do?" He swept his thumb across her cheek, catching several tears. "You're going to carry on, just like Quinn would expect you to do. You're going to do your job, you're going to enjoy your life, you're going to honor Quinn."

Honor Quinn. Kyra curled her hands around Jake's shirt. "I'm going to find The Player. He's still out there spreading evil, tormenting me."

# *THE TRAP*

---

## *Carol Ericson*

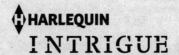

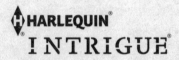

Recycling programs
for this product may
not exist in your area.

ISBN-13: 978-1-335-55516-8

The Trap

Copyright © 2021 by Carol Ericson

This edition published by arrangement with Harlequin Books S.A.

For questions and comments about the quality of this book,
please contact us at CustomerService@Harlequin.com.

Harlequin Enterprises ULC
22 Adelaide St. West, 40th Floor
Toronto, Ontario M5H 4E3, Canada
www.Harlequin.com

**Printed in U.S.A.**

**Carol Ericson** is a bestselling, award-winning author of more than forty books. She has an eerie fascination for true-crime stories, a love of film noir and a weakness for reality TV, all of which fuel her imagination to create her own tales of murder, mayhem and mystery. To find out more about Carol and her current projects, please visit her website at www.carolericson.com, "where romance flirts with danger."

Visit the Author Profile page at Harlequin.com.

# CAST OF CHARACTERS

*Jake McAllister*—This LAPD homicide detective is not only on the trail of a fourth copycat killer, he's close to unmasking the original serial killer, The Player, but to do so means risking the life of the woman he loves.

*Kyra Chase*—A victims' rights advocate with a traumatic past, she's eager to put that past behind her but she must face her biggest fear first—a confrontation with the man who murdered her mother twenty years ago and who now wants to kill her.

*Roger Quinn*—The retired LAPD homicide detective kept a secret for twenty years and now that he's dead, his secret has been exposed...putting his surrogate daughter in danger.

*Carlos Castillo*—An LAPD captain, he shared Quinn's secret for years; revealing it might blow the lid off The Player case, but it could also end his career.

*Dr. Shai Gellman*—This hypnotherapist is trying to help Kyra recover her traumatic memories, but he's putting them both in danger the closer they get to the truth.

*The Player*—This serial killer was able to avoid detection for years and even command his own cadre of copycats, but the witness he left behind is about to bring him down—unless he gets to her first.

# *Prologue*

Rule number one. Leave no witnesses.

Their eyes locked. He dropped the dead woman from his arms and took a tentative step toward the onlooker peering from behind the bush. The eyes glowing at him from the darkness widened and looked like a deer's in the crosshairs. The owner of those eyes took flight.

He glanced at the prey crumpled at his feet, and with rule number one pounding in his head, he took off after the witness, the plastic garbage bag encasing his body crackling with each step. He loped through the trees, gun dangling at his side. He'd needed the gun to force Ashley into his car, but he'd strangled her with gloved hands according to the playbook.

As he ran, twigs snapped back in his face, needling into his flesh. He thrashed about for several minutes, but he couldn't find a trail, or any clues as to which direction the person had run.

Had he…or she…even seen him? The body?

Tipping his head back, he surveyed the moonless sky between the treetops. Threatening clouds had been hovering over LA all day, even squeezing out a few drops of rain here and there. He'd been using a flashlight to dispose of Ashley's body and had switched it off when he heard the crack of a branch.

Maybe this person was no witness at all. He tugged the cap lower over his face. And maybe he was leaving evidence by chasing this person through the trees. He bent over, hands on his knees, his sweaty palms sticking to the plastic, his breath heaving in his chest.

At the sound of a car engine, he jerked his head up. Too late. Whoever it was had gotten away and might be calling the police right now.

He swung around and stumbled back to the clearing near the trail where he'd left Ashley. Less time now to complete his mission. He'd totally messed up his first kill, but he was determined to finish the job.

Ashley lay where he'd left her, undisturbed. He rolled her onto her back and swept the dark hair from her face. The previous copycat, Mitchell Reed, had selected his victims based on their appearance—brunettes with long hair who looked like some chick who'd jilted him in college. Pathetic loser.

He didn't care what they looked like. All

women were whores, just like his mother. He never got jilted. He was the one who did the jilting. He used them, took their money and left. But he never killed them. That would be breaking rule number four. Don't ever murder someone you know. The first copycat, Jordy Lee Cannon, had broken that rule. Pathetic loser.

As the past deeds of the previous copycats ran through his head, he'd been arranging Ashley's body into a position that would facilitate the rest of his tasks. He swept aside the plastic bag and pulled the playing card from his jacket and placed it between her lips. Eyes open or closed? He couldn't remember, so he left hers staring into the cloudy sky.

He fished the box cutter from the front pocket of his jeans and circled to Ashley's left side. Holding her wrist down with one hand, he used the box cutter to slice off her pinky finger. Blood spurted into the carpet of leaves beneath her hand. He dropped the finger in a baggie and sealed it.

A trophy for The Player.

They'd all done it. Severing the little finger of the victims' left hand had not only sent a message to law enforcement that The Player was back—if only by proxy—but also afforded The Player his trophy of choice. He'd be mailing Ashley's finger to a PO box. The other copycats had probably used a different PO box.

He shrugged. A small price to pay. He already had his souvenir of the kill, so he turned from the body to start his climb back to his car.

As he pivoted, he caught sight of the bush where he'd spotted someone hiding. What had that person been doing here at this time of night and alone?

He crept behind the bush and crouched, poking his head to the side to get a view of Ashley. Couldn't even tell that it was a body of a human. And where were the cops? Where was the outcry? The person had seen nothing of consequence.

He put his hands on the ground to hoist himself up, and his palm dug into something hard. He felt around the damp bed of twigs and leaves, and his fingers curled around a small bottle.

He picked up the clean prescription pill bottle and brought it close to his face. As he read the name on the bottle, his mouth stretched into a smile.

He now knew the identity of the witness—and now he could follow rule number one.

# Chapter One

Kyra perched on the edge of Quinn's love seat, the one she'd helped Charlotte pick out when she remodeled the Venice house, her hands clasped, her legs bouncing up and down, her face stiff. If Jake kept rubbing a circle on her back, he'd rub a hole right through to her spine.

When the coroner hitched the gurney onto its wheels, something broke inside her. She flung herself off the cushion and dropped to her knees next to Quinn's lifeless body ready to be transported away forever. "He can't be dead. Are you sure? Are you sure he's dead?"

Even as the words left her lips in a strained, high-pitched tone, she knew the truth. Quinn was gone, the only father she'd ever known.

"Kyra, let me take you away. You've been here long enough. You can't do anything for Quinn now. You gave him everything at the end. He's with Charlotte."

Kyra hadn't shed a tear yet—not when they

walked into Quinn's house and found him on the floor, not when she cradled his head in her lap as Jake told her Quinn had no pulse, not when Jake called 911, not when the EMTs pronounced him dead of a suspected coronary. Now her throat closed and her eyes ached, and when Jake pulled her up and crushed her to his chest with one arm, she buried her head against his shoulder and the floodgates opened.

She sagged against Jake as the wheels of the gurney spun out of the house. Quinn would never return to this house he'd shared with Charlotte, the house that had been her refuge when she'd been a mixed-up foster kid.

With the emergency personnel gone, the house creaked and sighed. The seawater lapped against concrete barriers that kept it away from the houses that hugged the banks of the canal. It seemed to whisper, "Charlotte, Charlotte." Is that what Quinn heard when he sat on his porch alone?

Jake stroked her hair. "I'm so sorry. I know Quinn was everything to you, as you were to him. He was so proud of the woman you've become. You couldn't have made him any happier."

She raised her head from the shirt she'd stained with her tears and took in the small house with a watery gaze. "Nothing will ever be the same again."

"Nothing ever is."

She balled her fist against her stomach. "What am I going to do?"

"What are you going to do?" He swept his thumb across her cheek, catching several tears. "You're going to carry on, just like Quinn would expect you to do. You're going to do your job. You're going to enjoy your life. You're going to honor Quinn."

Honor Quinn. Kyra curled her hands around Jake's shirt. "I'm going to find The Player."

Jake's body stiffened. "I don't think Quinn would want you to go down that path."

"Really?" She released her hold on Jake's shirt and paced to the sliding glass door that led from Quinn's kitchen to a deck over the canal. She stared at the moonlight cascading across the water.

"The Player was Quinn's one failure as a homicide detective. The Player murdered my mother, along with four other women, he encouraged and inspired three copycat killers—that we know of— and he's still alive. He's still out there spreading evil, tormenting me, and Quinn learned that truth a few weeks ago." She whipped around, a steely resolve replacing the sorrow that had sapped her strength over an hour ago. "That's *exactly* what Quinn would want me to do."

Jake opened his mouth, snapped it shut, took

a step toward her, stopped. "Before we get out of here, do you know if Quinn had an attorney?"

"Terrence Hicks. Why?"

"I know Hicks. He specializes in financial planning for cops. Used to *be* a cop." Jake spread his hands as if to encompass the house. "You should contact him to let him know about Quinn's death, although when a giant in law enforcement like Quinn passes, everyone knows."

"I think I have Hicks's card." Her gaze darted around the room. "I—I can't go through any of Quinn's stuff right now."

"Of course not." Jake crossed to the front door and removed the keys Kyra had left there when they first entered Quinn's house and saw his body. "Let's lock up and get something to eat."

She widened her eyes and crossed her arms over her midsection. "There's no way I can eat anything."

"Do you want me to take you home? Do you want to be alone?"

The old Kyra would've given an emphatic yes to that question, but the new and improved Kyra heard something in Jake's voice. She peered at him through her lashes, still wet with tears.

He bobbled her key chain in one hand while holding on to the doorjamb with the other, his neck stiff and his jaw tight. He'd lost Quinn, too. The two of them had gotten close, shared a bond as homicide detectives. Jake revered the old detective, but had a soft spot for him, too. He'd miss Quinn almost as much as she would.

Taking a deep breath, she straightened her spine and walked toward Jake. She wrapped her arms around his waist and said, "I want to be with you."

He dropped his head and kissed the top of hers. "I was hoping you'd say that. I don't want to go home alone. I want to talk about Quinn."

They wound up at her apartment in Santa Monica, much closer to Quinn's Venice house than Jake's place high in the Hollywood Hills. Jake ordered a pizza on the way, and by the time they and the food got to her place and Jake had opened a bottle of wine for her, she managed a few bites.

She brushed the crumbs from her fingertips over a paper plate. "The coroner will do an autopsy, right?"

"Yeah, but we know he had heart disease, already had two stents, and the EMTs indicated a coronary was likely." He pinged the side of her wineglass with his fingernail. "More wine?"

"Yes, please." As she watched the ruby-red liquid swirl into her glass, she asked, "Did anyone check for signs of forced entry?"

She felt Jake's eyes on her, probing, so she grabbed the slice of pizza on her plate and forced herself to take another bite.

"I did—everything locked up tight from the inside, not even a window cracked open. He probably closed up against the rain earlier in the day." He toyed with the crust on his plate. "No signs of a struggle. No defensive wounds on his hands. I did my due diligence as a detective before the first responders got there. What are you suggesting?"

The bite of pizza felt like sawdust in her mouth, so she washed it down with another gulp of wine. "I'm suggesting what any good detective might suggest, given Quinn's status at the LAPD. A retired detective with one cold case on his record, a cold case that has gotten hot in the past several months due to the copycats emulating The Player, and an admission by Quinn that The Player was still alive and directing the copycats."

"We think that's the case, or at least some of us do." He held up his hands in defense. "I believe he is, but it can't be verified."

"Quinn told us about information the copycats' puppet master passed along to them, information only The Player could've known. Then we have Mitchell Reed, Copycat Three, who kidnapped your daughter and was willing to exchange her for me—to please The Player."

Jake squeezed his eyes closed for a second, most likely remembering the moment he realized a serial killer had snatched his daughter. "We think that's why he wanted to make the trade, but The Player never showed up to claim you, did he?"

"I don't think you gave him enough time. You tracked Copycat Three down through Fiona's burner phone and rushed in there to save my life." She wiped her fingers on a crumpled napkin, and then took his hand. "I think that's about the third or fourth time you've come to my rescue."

"You saved my daughter. I'm never going to forget that." He brought her hand to his lips and pressed a kiss against the back of it.

"I'd do it all over again, but I couldn't save Quinn, could I?"

"From a heart attack? No, although you tried your best. You did more than his own doctor did, monitoring his diet—" he lifted his beer "—his alcohol."

"I shouldn't have allowed him to have any." Her bottom lip quivered and she tossed back some more wine.

"Quinn was a grown man. He did what he wanted, lived life on his own terms. Can't ask for more than that." He raised his bottle. "To Quinn."

"To Quinn." Her nose stung, and she glugged down the remainder of the wine.

Jake tipped the neck of his beer bottle at her. "You'd better slow down yourself or you're gonna end up in a world of hurt. You're not fooling me with those little nibbles of pizza. You have nothing in your stomach but red wine sloshing around in there. So eat up, or back away from the booze."

Sniffling, she surveyed him through watery eyes. "Oh, God. Is that how I sounded with Quinn? Because it's really annoying."

He rolled his eyes to the ceiling. "That's exactly how you sounded with Quinn, but it must've sounded more lovable coming from you because he complained, but he didn't mind—he didn't mind anything about you."

A tear rolled down her cheek. "He was my savior. Do you know, he's the one who personally took me to the Department of Children and Family Services when my mother had been murdered? I was covered in blood and..."

"Wait. I thought your mother had been strangled like all the rest."

"She had been, but during the struggle, because my mom fought like hell, she grabbed a vase and it broke on the floor. She cut herself on it, and I cut myself on it when I discovered her body the next morning. When the police showed up after I called 911, I was hiding in my bedroom. Then Quinn showed up, and I just knew everything was going to be okay."

"DCFS should've allowed him and Charlotte to adopt you. For all the issues that may have presented, how is it not better than foster care?"

Kyra lifted her shoulders. She'd been through

this with Quinn and Charlotte a million times. It didn't change a thing—didn't change that she'd lived in more foster homes than she cared to remember, culminating in the one where she'd killed a foster father in self-defense and to protect the younger girls in the home.

But Jake knew all about her sordid past, and it hadn't scared him off. When her phone buzzed, she blinked, wondering where the sound was coming from. Jake had been right about the two-plus glasses of wine on an empty stomach, but she was entitled to numb the pain.

Jake handed her the phone. "It's Billy."

"Why is your partner calling me?" After staring dumbly at the display for a few seconds, she answered. "Hi, Billy."

"Hey, Kyra. I heard about Quinn. Just want to let you know how sorry I am. If there's anything I can do for you, let me know."

Fresh tears spilled from her eyes. "Thank you, Billy. Do you want to talk to J-Mac? He's right beside me."

"That's where he should be, baby. No, I don't need to talk to him. Just called to offer my condolences on your loss and make sure you're doing okay, but if J-Mac's with you, I know he'll take care of you."

She thanked Billy again and ended the call. "I guess the word is out about Quinn's death."

"I knew it wouldn't take long." He held up the bottle. "More wine? Warm bath? You should eat more, but I'm not going to force you. Something besides pizza?"

"I'm okay." She stroked the cheek of the man who would stick by her through anything. He'd already proved that, and Quinn had approved of Jake. Quinn had had plans for them and their future, hers and Jake's—marriage, children. Now Quinn wouldn't be there to share in their future. Maybe those plans would all fall apart now.

"I do have one request."

"I will feed Spot if he comes meowing at your door."

She lifted a corner of her mouth, the closest she could come to a smile right now. "That, too, but could you stay the night? Just hold me? I couldn't bear waking up in the middle of the night alone and thinking about Quinn."

"I will absolutely spend the night with you. Like I said earlier, I don't much feel like being alone, either."

Her phone buzzed again, and she glanced at it, still clutched in her hand. "It's Captain Castillo. Hello, Captain."

"Hello, Kyra. We heard about Quinn. I'm—I'm devastated. Such a loss. I'm so sorry."

"Thank you, Captain Castillo. It was a shock finding him on the floor like that."

Castillo paused. "Heart attack? That's the word, and I know he had his difficulties."

"That's what it looks like now, but they're going to do an autopsy."

"They are?" Castillo's voice cracked and Kyra glanced at Jake.

"Jake said they probably would, given who he was."

"He's right. They probably will." Castillo cleared his throat. "Let me know if you need anything. Anything at all, anything the department can do for you."

"I will. Thanks again, Captain." He ended the call, and Kyra set the phone next to her paper plate, the cheese on her pizza hardening into an unappetizing glob. Her stomach gurgled. "That was nice of him."

"Castillo and Quinn always shared that bond of being the first ones at the scene of your mother's murder."

"Were they?" She tilted her head.

"Castillo was working patrol at the time. He's the one who responded to your 911 call. As soon as he walked into your mother's house, he called Quinn because he knew they had another one of The Player's victims on their hands. Quinn was nearby, so the two of them were at the house alone with you…and your mother's body for several minutes before the hordes showed up. I guess you left the bedroom for Quinn, but you wouldn't come out for Castillo."

"That's weird. I'm sure I read that, but I don't even remember. I knew Castillo had worked the case with Quinn, but I just thought he was on the original task force."

"Yeah, he was. After your mother's death, Quinn asked Castillo to join the task force. Castillo's career took off after that. From what I heard, it never hurt to have Detective Roger Quinn in your corner."

"And now he's never going to be in anyone's corner again. Certainly not mine." She dropped her head to her hands.

Jake lightly squeezed the back of her neck. "I'm in your corner now—and I'm not going anywhere."

She wouldn't be able to answer without bursting into tears again, so she just pressed her body close to his.

Spot's meows broke the spell, and Jake pushed off the couch. "I'm going to feed this mangy cat. Why don't you get ready for bed? I'll clean up everything here and join you later."

Kyra dipped her head and rose woozily from the couch. Her eyelids drooped and she silently thanked that bottle of cabernet. Without it, she never would've been able to sleep tonight.

As Jake bustled through her kitchen, she

brushed her teeth and washed her face with cool water. No need to remove her makeup. Her tears had already done that job. She smeared on some night cream, shed her clothing and crawled between the sheets.

Her eyes grew heavy, waiting for Jake to join her. Then the harsh ring of his work phone jolted her awake.

His body shifted beside her as he removed his arm from her waist. She peered over his shoulder at the digital clock and realized with a start that she'd drifted off and had slept through the whole night.

Jake's voice mumbled a hello. The mattress bounced as he shot up against the headboard. "You're kidding. Tell me you're kidding."

Rubbing her eyes, Kyra struggled to sit up, her hand squeezing Jake's bicep. "What? What's going on?"

Had they found out something about Quinn's death? Something suspicious?

Jake growled into the phone. "When will it end? When will this end? I'm on my way."

He said goodbye and tossed his phone onto the nightstand. Then he twisted around and cupped her face with one hand. "We have another copycat killer. Our fourth."

Kyra clutched the covers in her fists. "He's taunting Quinn—even in death."

## Chapter Two

Jake navigated the trail on the way to the body's dump site more sure-footed than he usually was, as he hadn't bothered to return home to change into a suit. The soles of his running shoes crunched the pebbles and twigs that littered the path beneath him.

No place to park a car here, so the killer must've carried the victim from the parking area almost a half a mile away. Strong. Bold. Sure of himself.

Kyra functioned as the task force's victims' rights advocate and all-around hand-holder and typically accompanied him to a crime scene, but he'd convinced her to stay behind today. On the heels of Quinn's death, she didn't need to be out here thinking about the one who escaped Quinn's net twenty years ago, the one who killed her mother.

He beat his partner to the scene, even though it had taken him almost an hour to reach the Angeles National Forest from Kyra's apartment in Santa Monica. As he tromped down the trail toward the yellow tape beckoning him through the trees, he caught the scent of pine that wafted down from the higher elevations of the park. The sun still dappled the ground between the leaves swaying above, but a distinct chill in the air had Jake hunching into his jacket.

The patrol officers guarding the body stood at attention when he approached. He didn't recognize them. The Angeles National Forest, the site of several dumped bodies over the years, didn't fall into the jurisdiction of LAPD's Northeast Division, but LA County's entire law enforcement world knew to call in the Copycat Player Task Force.

The name of the task force had morphed with the three different killers it had investigated and brought to a rough justice. They'd dubbed Jordy Lee Cannon, the first copycat, the Copycat Player for mimicking the MO of The Player. Little did they know at the time, they'd have three more killers terrorizing women in LA. The second killer, Cyrus Fisher, had earned the name Copycat 2.0, and they'd taunted the third copycat, Mitchell Reed, by calling him Copycat Three.

However, once they'd learned that the original serial killer, The Player, was responsible for encouraging and leading this new crop of killers, they'd decided to go back to Copycat Player for the task force name. In Jake's mind, he'd call this new guy Copycat Four. He just had no words or snappy nicknames left in his arsenal for this wave of evil.

He shook hands with the officers and then slipped on a pair of gloves. "Who discovered the body?"

Officer Llewellyn, a short stocky guy with a blond mustache, jerked a thumb over his shoulder at the emergency vehicles that had crowded the trailhead. "Two sanitation workers."

Glancing at the ground covered in a thick carpet of leaves, twigs and berries, Jake asked, "Any footprints?"

Llewellyn spoke again. "Not that we noticed, sir. No tire tracks, either, except for the sanitation truck's, but then, a car making its way down here in the middle of the night might be noticed."

"I figured he must've parked farther down and hiked here. Cameras on the parking lot?" He hadn't noticed any and Llewellyn's partner confirmed.

"No cameras, sir."

"Okay, thanks. Just keep the press out. I'm expecting my partner, and then we'll let the forensics team get to work." Jake ducked under the tape the officers had strung up between three trees and a stubby bush, keeping his eyes trained to the ground.

The officers had been correct. The thick carpet of dead plant life yielded no footprints or impressions when you walked on it. When Jake reached the lifeless body of the young brunette, he circled her. The queen of hearts protruded from her mouth and her left hand lay palm up, missing its little finger.

All the other copycats had taken their own trophies, and now the task force knew that the killers must've been sending the severed finger to The Player. He had to be getting some vicarious pleasure from this, but Jake knew the fingers from the other killers couldn't compare to the ones The Player had taken for himself twenty years ago.

He left the card in place for the crime scene photographer and crouched next to the body to verify the cause of death. With a gloved finger, he flicked a lock of hair from the woman's throat to reveal a necklace of deep purple bruising. Strangulation, but did her killer also use drugs to incapacitate her? The first copycat had relied on drugs to get women into his car. The second killer had attacked while his prey slept. The third had used the victims' natural state of intoxication to overpower them.

Footsteps crunched the ground, and Jake jerked his head to the side. Billy, dapper in a navy blue suit and pocket square, shook out a pair of gloves as he approached. His partner had obviously spent the night at his own place, and he'd had time to dress for work. They didn't call him Cool Breeze for nothing.

Stopping a few feet away from the body, Billy surveyed the area, his nostrils flaring, no doubt taking in every fallen leaf and every broken twig. Then he continued toward Jake and crouched beside him. "How's Kyra holding up?"

"She's doing okay. I told her to take the day off, but when she heard about this murder, she said Quinn would've wanted her to continue her work."

"She's probably right." Billy lifted the woman's left wrist to inspect the gaping wound on her hand, and her charm bracelet tinkled. "Bastard. Another woman murdered on The Player's orders on the very day Quinn dies. That's a slap in the face, man."

A muscle at the corner of Jake's eye throbbed. "The Player wouldn't have known about Quinn's death yet. Besides, we don't know if he's giving his minions the precise day for a killing or not."

"But we know he's directing them." Billy's jaw tensed for a second.

Jake rose, brushing his hands against his jeans. "Are there people on the task force still saying that the person orchestrating these murders is not necessarily The Player?"

Billy gave a sharp nod. "Me? I'm gonna go with Detective Roger Quinn's instincts and knowledge of the case. He made it clear that nobody could've known about the yellow diamond wedding ring missing from one of The Player's victims except The Player himself."

"Then we'll proceed accordingly, because I believe it, too." Jake pointed to the ground leading away from the body toward a denser area of the forest. "You see a little disturbance in the pattern of the detritus here?"

"If by detritus, you mean the stuff on the ground? Yeah." Billy joined him and stirred the accumulation of leaves, bark and stems with the gleaming toe of his shoe. "Not a trail, exactly, but a disturbance of some sort."

Jake followed the disruption of the material on the soil surface toward a bush, where it seemed to veer off toward the left. "Could he have walked this way for some reason?"

Billy answered, "Maybe he thought this would be a better place to dump the body and then changed his mind—too secluded."

"Maybe. I'd like to get a couple of uniforms to follow this path, if they can see it. I'm not losing my mind, am I?" Jake fingered a twig, freshly snapped from another bush. "Looks like someone went through this area not too long ago."

"You are not losing your mind. I see it, too, and you know I'm no outdoorsman skilled at tracking."

"Yeah, you're not exactly Daniel Boone." With his gaze pinned to the forest floor, Jake followed a route through the trees and bushes that someone had traversed recently. A few pieces of trash— food wrappers, a trashed sock, even a few old cigarette butts—littered the area, but the stuff had been around forever.

Billy whistled behind him. "I found something."

Jake spun around and charged toward Billy, who was holding up a piece of white paper. "It's not old, is it?"

Waving the paper, Billy said, "It's a receipt— from two days ago."

Jake clapped his partner on the back. "Daniel Boone ain't got nothing on you, brother."

KYRA SMOOTHED A hand down the thighs of her gray slacks and straightened her shoulders as she walked into LAPD's Northeast Division. It seemed weird coming here, knowing she wouldn't get to mull over her workday and the murders with Quinn later. She had a hard time remembering he was gone from her life forever.

No. She pressed a hand against her heart. He'd always be here, with her always. She sniffed and shoved her sunglasses to the top of her head. She waved at the officer manning the front desk and jogged upstairs to the task force war room.

She poked her head inside. Jake and Billy hadn't made it back from the crime scene yet, but by the way everyone buzzed around the room, she knew they had a fourth copycat killer on the loose.

As she scooted a chair up to her desk and pulled out her laptop, her phone rang. She glanced at the unknown number before she answered. "Hello?"

"Is this Kyra Chase?"

"It is. Who's this?"

The person on the other end of the line sighed. "I hoped this was the right number. This is Terrence Hicks. I'm Roger Quinn's attorney."

"Yes, I know. Quinn told me years ago he'd retained you to handle his estate planning. He gave me your card."

"I'm sorry that we finally have to meet this way. Quinn thought very highly of you...no, more than that. He loved you like a daughter."

Kyra's nose tingled again and she snatched a tissue from the box on her desk. "I—I was going to call you."

"I'm sorry to intrude on your grief, but I know Quinn would've wanted me to contact you as soon as possible." Hicks paused. "You know, Quinn left almost everything to you. You're his primary beneficiary."

"I know he wasn't that close to his sister's children, and Charlotte didn't have any nieces and nephews." Kyra chewed her bottom lip. "I suppose that means the Venice house."

"The house in Venice and the cabin in Big Bear. Back in the day, Quinn and Charlotte liked to go up to the mountains for a little skiing in the winter, a little fishing in the summer."

"I remember that cabin."

"Well, it's yours now. When can we meet, Ms. Chase? I can come out to you. There's no will to file. Quinn had a living trust, and you're the beneficiary. Clean and simple."

"Please call me Kyra." She tapped her phone's calendar and perused her appointments. She'd had two patients from her practice cancel on the same afternoon. "I have some availability tomorrow afternoon, if that works."

"I will clear my calendar for you. Quinn was my favorite client."

When she ended the call, Kyra drummed her fingers against her phone. Quinn had always told her he planned to leave her the house in Venice. She'd loved that house, but she didn't know if she'd be able to live there without Quinn or Charlotte.

She entered her appointment with Terrence Hicks into her phone and flipped open her laptop. As she launched her email, Jake and Billy strode into the room. Jake looked fresh in a charcoal suit and dark blue shirt. He and Billy must've stopped off at his place on the way over here.

Jake clapped his hands. "Listen up, everyone. Yes, it's true. We have a fourth copycat killer. Body dumped in the Angeles National Forest, no identification yet, but Cool Breeze here is going to get started on the missing person reports, and he needs a couple of people to help him. In the meantime, we found a receipt from a Walmart in Glendora—time-and date-stamped, so we can pull the video. As long as those cameras are working, we should be able to identify the owner of this receipt quickly."

Someone yelled out, "You think it's the killer?"

"Might be." Jake held up his hand. "Also, as you probably know, retired detective Roger Quinn passed away yesterday, suspected coronary. We'll keep you posted on the funeral. Let's honor Quinn and nail this guy like the others... and The Player who's giving them their marching orders. No briefing today. I gotta get going on this footage."

Kyra said a little prayer that the store's cameras would lead them right to the killer. A receipt at the dump site might not be enough to

file charges, but once the detectives had someone in their sights, collecting evidence and tying
that someone to the victim and the crime scene
made things easier. They'd have his car and his
home to search.

Several minutes later, Jake stopped by her desk
and perched on the edge. "Are you doing okay?
You really shouldn't be here today."

"I'm all right. I'd rather be here where Quinn
had his second home than at my apartment by
myself." She dabbed her nose with the crumpled
tissue on her desk. "I got a call from Terrence
Hicks already."

"He's fast. What did he tell you?"

"Nothing I didn't already know. Quinn had a
living trust and left me everything."

"You're going to have to go through that Venice house—whether you intend to sell it or keep
it. Quinn has a lot of junk in there."

She covered her eyes briefly with her hand.
"I'm not looking forward to that task."

"I'll help you." Jake rapped on the top of her
desk and stood up. "I'm going out to Glendora
to have a look at the footage. I called the store,
and they have it. They're going to pull it for me
before I get there."

Kyra brought up a map of LA County on her
computer and jabbed at the screen. "Glendora's

not that far from the Angeles Forest. Maybe he lives in that area."

"We'll find out, and then we'll unearth everything about this guy."

She called after his squared shoulders. "Good luck."

After Jake's announcement and departure from the room, the task force members got to work. They'd gone through this routine with three other killers, and now it had become sad second nature.

Kyra still had follow-up to do with the families of the previous victims. The pain didn't evaporate just because their loved ones' killers had been apprehended and in all three cases had died. As she knew all too well, it remained a terrible wound that eventually scabbed over. Then, when you least expected it, that scab could be ripped off by a memory, a smell, a song.

Her phone buzzed and she jumped. Terrence Hicks had a few more questions for her in anticipation of their meeting. She didn't like talking to him because it brought Quinn's death home. When she worked, she could forget about yesterday, forget she had found Quinn unresponsive on the floor of his house when she and Jake were supposed to be joining him for dinner.

When she ended the call with Hicks, Captain Castillo sidled up to her desk. "Are you doing okay? Another copycat killing on the heels of

Quinn's death is almost too much to take—for all of us."

"We'll get him this time, Captain…both of them, the fourth copycat and the man who's directing him."

"With Jake and Billy leading the way, I have no doubt." Castillo's already worried forehead creased further. "Are you going to plan Quinn's funeral? Contact the department if you need any help. We pull out all the stops for one of our own."

"I will, and I'm sure Terrence Hicks can assist with that, too."

Castillo's eyebrows shot up to his curly salt-and-pepper hair. "Hicks? You called Hicks already?"

Her cheeks warmed with the implication. "He called me this morning. He'd heard about Quinn's death and wanted to set up an appointment with me."

"Good." Castillo stroked his chin. "Terrence is a good guy. He'll carry out Quinn's wishes to the T. He'll know how to work with the department for the funeral, too."

Hunching forward, she said, "When is the medical examiner going to do Quinn's autopsy?"

Castillo's dark eyes widened. "I know you mentioned an autopsy before, but is it really necessary? I thought he died of a heart attack. He had a history of heart disease, a couple of stents."

"Jake told me that because of who Quinn was, they'd perform an autopsy."

Castillo asked, "Is that what you want?"

Kyra smacked a hand against her chest. "What I want? Do I have a say?"

"As the next of kin and his sole heir, I think you can request they bypass the autopsy." A muscle at the corner of Castillo's eye twitched. "Do you want the autopsy?"

"Absolutely." She wasn't going to admit to Captain Castillo that she had her suspicions about Quinn's death. Quinn did have heart disease, but he'd been doing so much better lately. The meds thinned his blood and kept his blood pressure down—even in the midst of the copycat killings. He hadn't been complaining about his health… and he'd recently made the discovery that his old nemesis, The Player, was alive and well and orchestrating a new crop of serial killers.

Nodding, Castillo turned to go. "Then you'd better talk to the ME."

Jake had never made it back for lunch, and she'd grabbed a sandwich at her desk. He still hadn't returned by the time she started packing up to leave.

She'd noticed some activity at Billy's desk earlier and sauntered across the room after shoving her laptop in its case. She hung over his shoulder as he clicked through and sorted the photos of women who'd gone missing in LA County recently.

She asked, "Any luck?"

"No and no." His cursor hovered over the face of a dark-haired beauty with innocent eyes. He dragged her photo into a folder.

"Two no's? Is that for emphasis?"

"That's a no luck in ID'ing the victim yet, and no luck with that receipt."

Her fingers curled around the back of his chair. "You heard from Jake?"

"He found the person who made that purchase and had that receipt, but it's a woman—single, no boyfriend lurking in the background."

"That's a disappointment, but it could still lead to something. What was she doing out there, or was she even out there?"

"That's what we're going to find out. Jake ID'd her from the credit card info and called her in for an interview."

"That's progress. Did she wonder what it was all about?"

Billy shrugged, not taking his eyes from the monitor. "I didn't get that far in the convo."

"Okay, I'll leave you to it." Because Billy's own sister had gone missing, he had a passionate need to identify the murder victims as soon as possible. She patted his shoulder before gathering her things.

She trailed down the stairs to the lobby of the station. The shift change had already occurred, so the activity level had tapered off down here. As Kyra waved to the desk sergeant, she eyed a young woman sitting all alone in a chair by the window, the setting sun striking her red hair, creating a little glow around her head.

The woman held a crumpled tissue in her hand and periodically dabbed her nose, which practically matched the color of her hair. She had one thin leg encased in black denim curled around her other leg. She looked like a pretzel—a sad pretzel.

With her own loss painfully fresh, Kyra felt a kindred emotion stir in her breast, and she veered from her path to the door to the bereft woman.

Kyra crouched beside her and said, "Are you all right? Can I get you something?"

The redhead jerked, dropping her sodden tissue. "N-no. I'm all right. I mean, everything's wrong, but I'm okay."

Kyra raised her brows and jerked her thumb toward the front desk. "Have you been helped?"

"Oh, yes. I told him that I was here to see Detective McAllister."

Kyra's heart leaped. This must be the owner of the receipt. She took a quick glance around the room and scooted in closer to the woman. "You're the one who lost the receipt."

The woman's eyes widened, their shade of

green almost matching Jake's, and her face blanched, causing the freckles to stand out on her nose. "I—I did. Are you a cop?"

Kyra flushed and tossed back her ponytail. "No, but I'm working on the task force."

"Task force?" The woman's voice squeaked.

Kyra pressed her lips together. She'd said too much. Jake probably hadn't even told her where they'd found the receipt or why he needed to talk to her. She flicked her fingers in the air. "An LAPD task force. I know Detective McAllister. I can take you upstairs to wait for him, make you more comfortable, give you a little privacy."

"Oh, yes, please. I'd like that." She peered over her shoulder out the window, her green eyes wide. "Because I think I witnessed a murder."

## Chapter Three

Jake burst through the doors of the LAPD's Northeast Division, his stride long in direct correlation to his tardiness. He tripped to a stop when his gaze stumbled across Kyra sitting on a chair next to a blubbering redhead, Kyra's arm around the other woman's shoulders. He squinted. Was this someone connected to Quinn? Looked about two generations removed from Quinn's.

His step faltered as he approached the two women. "Is everything okay?"

Kyra patted the woman's hunched back. "Piper, this is Detective McAllister. Detective, this is Piper Moss. She's your witness."

Jake's eyes narrowed. He knew damn well who Piper Moss was. He was late to their appointment. But what the hell was Kyra doing with her and...? His heart slammed against his chest. "Wait. Witness?"

"That's right." Kyra dropped her voice, although the desk sergeant was the only one who had a chance of hearing anything over the couple screaming at each other in the corner.

Kyra continued. "Piper was in the Angeles National Forest last night...where she saw someone dump a body."

Jake had to fold his arms to keep himself from rubbing his hands together. Didn't seem the right move for the moment. "Thanks for coming, Ms. Moss. Let's go upstairs."

Piper made a grab for Kyra's hand. "Can she come, too?"

Kyra *did* have a way of insinuating herself into people's lives. She'd done a damn good job infiltrating his mind, body and soul. "Of course. Kyra is a therapist and victims' rights advocate. She works closely with the department."

"I need an advocate...and you can call me Piper."

Jake ushered Kyra and Piper up the stairs ahead of him. Had Kyra been able to extract the information out of Piper that she'd been in the Angeles National Forest last night, or had Piper come here to tell him that herself? She could've claimed that the receipt fell out of her purse somewhere. Why hadn't she come forward before his call?

When they reached an interrogation room, Jake herded them inside. "Can you tell us what happened last night, Piper?"

The young woman shot a quick glance at Kyra,

who gave her a barely perceptible nod. "I went to the Angeles National Forest last night to kill myself."

Jake had been scribbling on a notepad, and his pen went off the edge. "You were going to commit suicide out there?"

"Yes." Piper's lower lip trembled, and Kyra grabbed her hand with its stubby red fingernails.

"I'm sorry, Piper." Jake put down his pen. "Why would a young woman like you want to end your life?"

She lifted her narrow shoulders. "My brother died in a motorcycle accident last year, I got fired from my job a few months ago, my girlfriend broke up with me and I'm camping out on the couch of a friend. Life just sucks right now."

Jake had never been happier for Kyra's presence. Piper needed a level of comfort he didn't think he had in him. Kyra had saved him from uttering some stupid, useless homilies by offering Piper her heartfelt solace. Every word out of Kyra's mouth rang with a sincerity that couldn't be faked.

When Piper was able to meet Jake's eyes again, he said, "What were you going to do to yourself up there, Piper?"

"OD on pills." She ran a hand through her thick hair. "I know, so bourgeois."

Jake swallowed. He didn't realize methods of

suicide could be categorized by class. "Are you in danger of hurting yourself now?"

"No, what happened last night made me think twice about ending my life." Her thin frame shuddered.

"What did happen last night?" He picked up his pen.

"Can I ask you one question first?"

"Go ahead."

"How did you know I'd been in the forest? I know there aren't any cameras there. I checked." She snapped her fingers. "You asked about my trip to Walmart, didn't you? You must've found my receipt."

"That's exactly what happened. We were investigating a murder this morning and found your receipt. We thought it might be our killer."

"Until you saw me on the footage, right?" She tapped her chest twice with her flattened hand. "You know I didn't kill anyone."

"I didn't think you had, but I thought you might have a husband or a boyfriend who did."

"I don't have anyone." Her lower lip protruded, and Jake held his breath, waiting for another round of sobbing.

Kyra plucked a few tissues and handed them to Piper. "You don't have anyone right now, but you're here doing something incredibly brave."

Jake cleared his throat. "Let's get back to last

night. You were there to…kill yourself, and you saw someone with a body."

"That's right."

"Stop." Jake held up his hand. "Where did you park, and did you see any other cars there?"

"I parked in the lot near the trailhead, the Garcia Trail. Mine was the only car there. I wouldn't have parked there otherwise. I hiked down the trail, and was, you know, contemplating my crappy life. Then I heard noises coming from the other end of the trail, and I got scared. Weird, huh? I'm there to kill myself, but I'm afraid that someone else is going to do it first."

"Not weird at all." Jake splayed his hands on the table in front of him. "It was cloudy last night. How much did you see?"

"Not much. When I heard the person coming, I hid behind a bush. A man walked down the trail with something over his shoulder. He made a crinkling noise as he walked."

Jake cocked his head. "Crinkling?"

"I heard it when he chased me, too. Sort of sounded like a garbage bag."

"H-he saw you? He chased you?" Kyra put a hand to her throat.

Jake kept his face impassive and eased a slow breath from his mouth. "How soon after he got there did he notice you?"

"Pretty quickly. He walked up with the body

over his shoulder, looked around for a bit. He stopped in one spot, which, unfortunately for me, was right across from my bush. I must've made a sound because he jerked his head up and stared right at me."

"That's when you ran?"

"Took off like a rabbit." She tapped her fingers on the tabletop. "I got a head start on him, and I think that plastic bag he was wearing slowed him down. I was able to scramble up to my car and take off."

"You were very, very lucky."

"Gave me a new lease on life. All the stuff that happened, except for my brother, it doesn't seem so bad now. I could be that dead girl in the forest." Piper hugged herself, digging her fingers into her upper arms.

"What can you tell me about his appearance? I know it was dark, but height, weight, hair, clothing?"

Piper took a deep breath. "He was tall, or maybe that's because I was crouched down. He seemed big to me—not overweight but not skinny. He had a baseball cap on, dark, but I didn't see any words, pictures or letters on it. I couldn't see his clothes, but that's probably because he had a trash bag over his body."

Jake drilled the point of his pen into the piece of paper. That would explain why they hadn't found any fibers on the victims' clothing. "You're doing great, Piper."

Jake continued his interview with Piper. Her brush with danger had given her a new perspective on her life, so in a weird way, Copycat Four had saved a life just after he'd taken another.

Piper hadn't seen enough of the killer's face to help with a composite, so Jake slipped her a card and said, "If you remember anything else about this guy, anything at all, even if it seems minuscule, let me know."

"He's not going to know—" Piper glanced at Kyra "—I mean, nobody's going to know that I saw him, right?"

Jake shook his head. "I have no intention of telling the press that we have a witness."

"Okay, I feel better." She slumped in her chair. "That's why I didn't call the police to tell them what I saw. I was afraid. When I saw the news later that a body had been found right where I was, I figured I better tell someone. Really. I'm not just saying that because you called me first."

"I understand. It must've been frightening, but you're here now and you've been a big help."

"It's not just because I was scared, either. I didn't want to admit what I was doing there." Piper shoved a thumbnail between her teeth and worried it.

"Call me anytime, day or night, if you have

those feelings again." Kyra added her card to Jake's. "What pills were you going to use? Do you still have them?"

"Some antianxiety meds I've been on and off since my brother's death." Piper unzipped the purse slung across her body and resting in her lap. She shoved her hand into the largest compartment. "I do still have them, but I haven't even taken one after my…encounter last night."

"I'm not saying you shouldn't have them if you legitimately need them for anxiety, but maybe you don't need to have so many of them. Are you currently seeing a psychiatrist?"

"No." Piper's eyebrows collided over her nose as she dug deeper into her purse. "My regular doctor prescribes them."

Piper swung her purse onto the table and dumped the contents. She began pawing through loose change, tubes of lipstick, a sticky breath mint and receipts. No wonder she'd lost one from her purse.

"Are you looking for your pills?" Kyra asked.

Her hands still splayed in the hodgepodge of items from her bag, Piper looked up, her eyes glassy and wide. "They should be here. They were in my purse last night, and I hadn't even left my friend's couch today until I came here."

Kyra slid a glance at Jake. "Could they be in your car?"

"My purse was zipped. I just opened that part of it now. I left my sunglasses in the car, and my keys and phone are in the outside pocket." Her chewed fingernails clawed into the table. "I dropped them there. I must've lost them last night. I remember I had them. I'd taken them out of my purse and when I heard that freak coming, I shoved them back into my purse. I bet I missed the opening and then I didn't zip up my purse and that's how the receipt flew out. I left my pill bottle there. Did you find it?"

Jake's mind had been racing along with Piper's narrative. "Just the receipt."

Grabbing the roots of her hair with both hands, Piper moaned and rocked forward. "He has them. He found them. He knows who I am."

"We don't know that for sure." Kyra rubbed a circle on Piper's back. "Jake?"

"We didn't find a pill bottle there. Otherwise, we would've been able to ID you a lot faster than through that receipt." Jake didn't bother to point out that Piper's address wouldn't be on that prescription label, but there would be enough information on it to track her down for someone savvy enough with computers or devious enough—and they knew this guy was both.

"Because he took it. He took it." Piper shoved the items on the table back into her purse, her hands shaking so badly that half the stuff wound up on the floor.

As Kyra bent over to pick up the items, Jake said, "Even if he gets your address, and I'm not saying he can't or won't, you're no longer living there, right? He's not going to track you down to your friend's house."

"My girlfriend still lives at my old place. The condo is in both our names." Piper grabbed her phone and scrolled through the display. "I've been trying to reach Erica all day. I wasn't too worried before because she keeps telling me not to call or text her and I've been trying to let her go, but I wanted to let her know what happened last night—not the suicide part, but the rest of it."

"We'll notify her." Jake kept his own voice calm in the face of Piper's rising hysteria and his own uneasiness.

"Forget that. I need to see her now. I need to warn her to be careful." Piper jumped up from the table, and her chair fell back.

"We're not going to let you go there alone. Right, Detective?" Kyra tipped her head toward the door.

Jake grabbed his notepad and pushed back from the table. Had he expected his day to end any differently? "Where's the condo?"

"I-it's in West Hollywood. Are you coming?"

"We're taking you there."

On the drive over, Kyra tried to talk Piper down, but the young woman's agitation increased the closer they got to the condo until she was practically bouncing around the back seat.

Jake parked in front of the pink stucco building on a street that housed similar condo complexes converted from apartments. He twisted in his seat. "Piper, you stay here with Kyra. I'll check on Erica and let her know what's going on. If she wants to talk with you, I'll call Kyra and you can come up. The way things stand between you two, we don't need to add a domestic dispute to your life."

When he got Piper's assent in the form of a sniffle and a drop of her head, Jake exited his vehicle and walked between the two stately palm trees that guarded the front door of the building. He buzzed the number Piper gave him, but nobody replied. He was about to use Piper's key on the front door when two men walking out held it open for him. So much for security.

He cruised past a bank of brass mailboxes and a few potted palms on his way to the elevator and rode it up to the third floor. A carpet hushed his footsteps as he read the numbers on the doors on his way down the hallway. When he reached Erica's, he knocked and took a step back, standing in full view of the peephole. As he fished his badge from his front pocket, he glanced down and noticed a dark scuff at the bottom of the door. He ran a finger along the doorjamb, looking for a break or splintered wood.

He knocked again, calling out, "Erica? I'm a detective with the LAPD. I need to talk to you."

He pulled Piper's key chain from his pocket. She was still on the title, and she'd given him permission to enter. He rapped his knuckles against the door again as he pushed it open.

His heart pounded when he stepped on some broken glass. As he ventured another few steps into the living room, his eye tracked from the upended coffee table to the lamp on its side to a cracked picture on the floor.

Erica had put up a good fight. His gaze rested on the body splayed across the couch.

She'd lost.

# Chapter Four

Kyra scrambled after Piper, her high-heeled boots doing her no favors, as Piper dashed up the stairwell of the condo building.

Jake could be having a civilized conversation with Erica right now and Piper's appearance might upset everything. Kyra's heels clanged on the steps after Piper's sure-footed ascent on a pair of Chucks. She heard the fire door squeal open above her, and she cursed silently. Jake had given her one job to do—keep Piper in the car.

The door slammed shut, the sound ringing down the stairwell. Panting, Kyra scaled the final staircase from the second to the third floor and shoved open the fire door. As she burst into the hallway, she saw Piper stumbling backward from the open door of a unit, her hands clapped over her mouth.

Despite the fear coursing through Kyra's body and weakening her knees, she raced forward, her heart hammering in her chest. As she drew closer to Piper, the woman dropped her hands and screamed through her gaping mouth.

Jake shot out into the hallway and hovered over Piper. "Don't go in there. You don't need to look at her. I've called 911."

Doors up and down the hallway either cracked or flew open, and heads popped out of the condos.

Jake waved his hands. "Police business. Stay inside for now, please."

When Kyra reached Piper, the younger woman threw herself into Kyra's arms and sobbed. "She's dead. She's dead. It's all my fault. I should've told her."

Meeting Jake's flashing eyes over Piper's head, Kyra murmured, "You couldn't have known. Nobody knew."

The phone Jake gripped in his hand rang, and he pivoted back into the condo. After speaking for a few seconds, he shouted over his shoulder. "The first responders are here. I'm going to let them up."

Piper shook her head. "It's no use. She's dead."

Squeezing Piper's arm, Kyra said, "They need to process the scene. They'll find this guy. Let's wait somewhere else while they do their jobs."

"I'm not leaving her." Piper dug her heels into the carpet and flattened her hands against the wall behind her.

The elevator dinged and the doors opened on two sheriff's deputies from West Hollywood and two EMTs.

Kyra waved at them from down the hall. "Over here."

Jake plunged back into the condo ahead of them, and Kyra could see him through the door talking to the deputies. This area belonged to the LA County Sheriff's Department, not the LAPD, but as Copycat Four was most likely Erica's killer, the task force would be involved.

With Jake no longer present, giving orders, a few of the residents wandered into the hallway and peppered Kyra with questions, as they stared at Piper pacing back and forth.

Kyra stopped twisting her fingers into knots and tried to look authoritative. "There's been an accident. The police will talk to you later."

Maybe someone had seen or heard something. Kyra had only gotten a peek into Erica's place, but it looked like there'd been some disruption. The killer had been reckless coming after who he thought was Piper, so he must've been desperate to shut her up.

The police would have to keep quiet about the motivation for this murder and never let the killer know he'd murdered the wrong woman. His witness was still alive and if not exactly well, she'd be out for vengeance.

Piper's mental state worried Kyra. The young woman had already been through so much. Would the death of Erica lead her to another suicide attempt? Piper hadn't seemed too serious about the first attempt, but you could never tell.

More cops poured out of the elevator, and one duo began approaching the neighbors. Kyra tried to tune in, but she couldn't hear their conversation other than a few gasps and a few mentions of Erica's name. She peered into the corner near the elevator and noticed the camera.

As Piper careened past her for the hundredth time, Kyra caught her arm. "Your car's still at the station. Can you call a friend? We can give you a ride home if you want to leave your car there. You shouldn't be alone."

Piper broke away from her and sank to the floor, her head on her knees.

Finally, Jake peeled away from the scene inside the condo. "We can take Piper back to her friend's place."

"That's what I told her." Kyra tipped her head toward the knots of people clustered up and down the hallway. "Did anyone hear anything?"

Jake dipped his head to hers. "Time of death appears to be in the afternoon. A lot of these people were working. The one guy who works at home is a film editor and had headphones on most of the day. One or two people work a night shift and could've been home during the time of the murder. We'll talk to them later."

"Did you notice the cameras?"

"Sheriff's department is on it now. They're going to send the footage to the task force tomorrow." His gaze slid to Piper on the floor, her chin to her chest, arms wrapped about her legs, and he whispered, "She needs to move."

"I'll get her going."

After much coaxing and assurances, Kyra and Jake convinced Piper to leave the building and got her back to the station. Her friend met them there and followed her back to his place after assuring Kyra he'd keep an eye on her.

Kyra slumped in her chair at her desk. "Did you ever think tracking down the owner of that receipt would lead to this?"

"It must've happened just as Piper said." Jake ran a hand through his hair. "She dropped her prescription bottle, the killer found it, tracked down her address and killed the person living there—only he killed the wrong person."

"I didn't want to ask you in front of Piper, but did he commit the murder like a copycat?" She folded her arms and tucked her hands at her sides. "Strangulation, playing card, severed finger?"

"Nope. I'm guessing he didn't want us to connect this murder with his ritualistic ones. Although he did strangle Erica, he used a cord instead of his hands. Looks like he stole some cash from her purse, probably to throw us off. He may not realize we've even spoken to Piper. We certainly haven't announced there was a witness this time."

"Do you intend to keep that out of the press?"

"As much as possible." Jake ambled back to his desk to pack up for the night.

They'd been gone so long with Piper, they had the Copycat Player task force room all to themselves. Now Kyra just wanted to get home and prepare for her meeting with Terrence Hicks tomorrow. "Does it look like Copycat Four might've left some evidence at Erica's place?"

"He left a mess. That's for sure. I'm counting on something to turn up." Jake hitched his bag over his shoulder. "The killer got in deep when he broke one of The Player's rules, one The Player never broke himself…leave no witnesses."

THE FOLLOWING DAY, Kyra didn't go into the station. She had clients to see at her office in Santa Monica. She'd been able to move one afternoon appointment to the morning to clear her schedule for Hicks, and now she checked the clock on her desk to see if she'd have time to pick up something to eat before Hicks's arrival at her apartment. She'd crammed all her work into the first half of the day and had missed lunch completely.

She'd offered to meet Hicks at his office in Century City, but he told her Quinn would be scowling down at him if he didn't make everything as easy as possible on her.

Jake had been able to contact the medical examiner on her behalf this morning to make sure he'd be performing an autopsy on Quinn. He'd assured Jake that was his plan all along. Not that Kyra expected a different cause of death from the heart disease that had plagued Quinn for the past several years, but what kind of detective's daughter would she be if she didn't make sure?

On the short drive from her office to her apartment, Kyra cruised past a deli and picked up a turkey sandwich. She ordered a second for Hicks, just in case. Quinn would be scowling down on *her* if she didn't treat his attorney right. She still couldn't believe she'd lost the only father she'd ever known, and her eyes blurred with tears on the rest of her way home.

When she got to her apartment, she shooed Spot, the stray cat, away from her door, dumped her purse on the low wall that separated her kitchen from the entryway, and placed a notepad, pen and her laptop on the coffee table.

As she wolfed down her sandwich and a diet soda, she kept her eye on the security footage from her phone. Jake had insisted she install security cameras around her apartment after The Player had gotten too close for comfort.

She didn't know the person taunting her with remnants of her past was The Player until recently, and the knowledge had made the teasing more sinister and frightening. He'd never attempted to physically harm her, but he hadn't put physical violence behind him. He'd killed twice to protect his interests—a homeless woman in Santa Monica who had done his bidding and a true crime blogger who'd gotten too close to one of The Player's copycats. Had he killed Erica, too? Had Jake even thought of that possibility?

When the doorbell rang, she jumped even though Terrence Hicks was right on time and she could see him standing at her door from her phone. She balled up the waxy paper from her sandwich and tossed it in the trash.

She opened the door on the compact attorney, his fit frame outfitted in a navy-blue suit, his bald pate gleaming and a tidy goatee accentuating his chin. He looked exactly like his pictures on the internet.

He thrust out his hand. "Ms. Chase, I'm Terrence Hicks. It's a pleasure to finally meet you after hearing about you from Quinn these past ten years."

"Kyra, remember?" She invited him inside and

offered him the sandwich, which he declined, and a diet soda, which he accepted.

She popped the tab on the can in the kitchen and poured the fizzing liquid over some ice in a glass as Terrence settled on the couch. She carried the drink to him and said, "Is this okay? We can work on the kitchen table if that's easier."

"This is fine." He took the glass from her hand and placed it on a coaster. Then he opened his own laptop next to hers and plopped a thick folder onto his lap. "Quinn did everything right. All his assets are in a living trust, and you are the sole beneficiary, except for a few charitable concerns and small items. His most valuable asset was his home in Venice, which, as you can imagine, is worth over two million dollars—and it's paid off."

Kyra glanced around the small apartment she'd been renting for more than five years. Should she move into Quinn's house? She pinned her hands between her knees. She couldn't imagine being there without him.

The transfer of Quinn's assets went smoothly. She signed where Terrence told her to sign, made a few decisions regarding taxes and even discussed Quinn's funeral arrangements. Terrence had all the right contacts at the LAPD and had already set things in motion.

An hour later, Terrence began to stuff the papers and legal documents back into his briefcase and mentioned Jake's name.

Kyra jerked her head up from shuffling through her own set of documents Terrence was leaving with her. "What about Jake?"

"Quinn altered his trust recently, leaving a few items to J-Mac. I haven't called him yet, but I plan to do that today."

"Quinn left Jake something in his will?" Kyra raised her eyebrows as she collected Terrence's empty glass. "He really *did* have expectations for us."

Terrence cracked a smile, his teeth white against his dark face. "I told you. Quinn had your future all mapped out for you."

"What did Quinn leave him, or am I not allowed to ask that?"

"A few weapons." Terrence reached into his briefcase and pulled out an envelope. "And this. I do have to place this in Jake's hand and I don't know what's in it, but I have some business at the Northeast Division and I can give it to him there."

She eyed the envelope suspiciously. "Ugh, I hope there's not some sort of care and feeding of Kyra Chase in there."

Terrence chuckled as he slipped the envelope in a side pocket of his bag. "It might be. Quinn worried about you."

"I know, and all that time I should've been

worrying about him." Kyra pressed a fist against her lips to stop the sob that threatened to escape.

Terrence placed a hand on her shoulder and gave it a gentle squeeze. "You took good care of Quinn. He told me himself."

"Thank you, Terrence. I'll be in touch about the funeral. The ME is doing an autopsy."

"I figured as much."

She walked Terrence to the door, and he stopped suddenly, digging into the pocket of his jacket. "I forgot to give you the keys to the houses."

"I have my own key to the house in Venice."

"I know that, but this makes it official." He dangled a key chain from his fingers and dropped it into her waiting palm. "Let me know what you plan to do with the house—move in or sell it. No hurry."

"Good, because I'll have to think about it."

When the attorney left, Kyra shook out some kibble into a bowl for the missing Spot, who'd left in a huff after she'd shunned him. As she passed through the kitchen, she snatched the extra sandwich from the fridge and curled up in front of the TV with a glass of wine.

Then she put on the next episode of the show she and Quinn had been watching together—a show he'd never finish—and drank deeply.

"WHAT DID HICKS WANT?" Captain Castillo strolled into the nearly empty task force war room and sat on the edge of Billy's desk. "Plans for Quinn's funeral?"

Jake glanced up from the thick envelope Hicks had left him, Quinn's bold writing scrawled across the front, and dropped it on his desk. "Yeah, we talked about that. There's a lot to do, but Hicks has gone through this before for other clients."

He didn't want to read any last words Quinn had for him in front of the captain.

Castillo's gaze flicked to the envelope before meeting Jake's eyes. "West Hollywood Sheriff's Department hasn't come up with much at the scene of Erica Fuentes's murder, have they?"

"They sent the footage over, and the guy knew he was on camera, because he avoided it as much as possible and wore a thick jacket, a hat and a hoodie. Can't tell much from that. He did have a box in his hands, as if he were a delivery guy. Maybe that's how he got her to open the door, and then he kicked it open once she cracked it. We don't see anything again until he leaves with the box under his arm and is able to avoid the cameras on his way out of the building. We checked for parking tickets on the street during that time, canvassed the neighbors, looked at other footage in the area—nothing."

Castillo picked at a cuticle. "You ever think this might be The Player cleaning up for one of his minions, like he did with that crime blogger?"

"Billy and I thought about it. Could be, but that still doesn't give us any more evidence than what we got."

"How's the real witness?"

"Hanging on. Kyra spoke with her over the phone today. She's more upset about the death of her girlfriend now than she is about witnessing that body dump." Jake shrugged into his jacket.

Castillo hopped off the desk. "Kyra doing okay?"

"She's fine. She wants to go to Quinn's house tomorrow, which I think is a little too soon, but once she makes up her mind, there's no stopping her. I guess it's progress. At first, she didn't think she'd ever be able to return to that house."

"That's a prime piece of property."

"It is." Jake raised his brows at the unusually loquacious captain, hoping he'd take the hint to wrap it up.

Castillo said, "I'll let you get going. Long days for everyone. Your daughter doing okay after the kidnapping?"

Jake swept Quinn's envelope from the desk and tucked it in the inside pocket of his jacket. "She's recovered. Maybe even learned a lesson or two—I know her mother and I learned a few things about social media accounts."

"It's a tough age. Not looking forward to going through that stage with my two youngest. When my older kids were teens, social media wasn't as pervasive."

"Gotta keep vigilant." Castillo was on his second marriage and had two young kids with this wife, although his older daughter was married and expecting Castillo's first grandchild. Jake had missed a lot of Fiona's childhood years, but was eager to experience it all with his and Kyra's children—if he could persuade her to go down that path with him.

Finally, Castillo made a move, and Jake walked out of the room with him, waving to a few of the officers staying behind. Everyone on a task force had a job to do, and some of that work was better suited to a quiet office and quiet phones.

Castillo peeled off at his own office, and Jake jogged down the stairs and exited the building. Before getting into his car, he sloughed off his jacket and snatched the envelope from the pocket. He slid behind the steering wheel of his unmarked sedan and slipped his thumb beneath the sealed flap of the envelope.

He pulled out several sheets of paper. One listed a description of some weapons Quinn was leaving to Jake. The second page contained a note from Quinn. In the note, Quinn explained to Jake that he had some files related to The Player locked away in a safe. He'd ended the note with a cryptic statement about how Jake would understand why he kept the file a secret once Jake looked through it.

The crease between Jake's eyebrows deepened when he got to the third sheet. He smoothed the paper over the steering wheel and studied the map Quinn had sketched—a real, live treasure map. Only X didn't mark the spot out in the desert or even in a storage unit like Kyra's foster brother had kept.

Quinn had buried his treasure under the floorboards of his house in Venice. Even more mysterious was Quinn's final directive that Jake not tell Kyra about this file. Jake's mouth got dry. It must be something horrendous about her mother's murder Quinn had never told her.

He'd follow Quinn's instructions to a T, but he'd have to figure out how he was going to lift up some floorboards in a room in a house that Kyra now owned.

THE FOLLOWING EVENING, after a full day of work and a quick bite to eat from a fish market on the Santa Monica Pier, Jake drove Kyra to Quinn's house to start looking around. Kyra wasn't planning to start packing up anything, but she did want to find a nice suit for Quinn's burial and get a feel for whether she could live in the house.

Jake didn't press the issue, but he was hoping she'd start thinking about the idea of moving in with him. She could still hang on to the Venice house and rent it out—but this wasn't the time or the place.

He parked his car as close to the canal walk streets as he could, conscious of Quinn's map tucked in the back pocket of his jeans as they crossed the bridge to the red door of Quinn's house—Kyra's house.

With shaky fingers, she inserted the key and turned the handle. Jake reached around her to push open the door.

Kyra hesitated on the threshold, clutching the key chain at her side, her gaze glued to the spot where they'd discovered Quinn's body.

Jake nudged her back gently. "I'm right behind you."

He followed her into the living room, and his nose twitched at the air, already musty even though the house had been empty just a few days. He didn't detect any odor of death and released a pent-up breath. "I'm going to open some windows and the back door just to get some air in here."

On his way to a window to yank up the sash, he glanced down at the hardwood floor beneath a throw rug in front of the fireplace—Quinn's secret hiding place.

As he grabbed the window, Kyra gasped behind him and he spun around.

Standing in front of a built-in bookcase, Kyra turned to him, her eyes wide and her face pale. "Someone's been here, Jake. Someone broke into Quinn's house."

# Chapter Five

Jake's eyebrows jumped to his hairline, but his face didn't reflect the panic she felt clawing at her chest. Didn't he see? If someone broke into Quinn's place, maybe that person was also responsible for Quinn's death.

Surveying the room, Jake said, "What makes you say that? Everything's shut up tight, or it was until I opened this window. The dead bolt on the front door was locked, wasn't it?"

She chewed her bottom lip and grabbed the two pictures from the bookcase. She thrust them in front of her. "These were out of place."

"Two pictures were out of place on a shelf and you jump to break-in?" Jake cocked his head. "That's a big leap. How do you know Quinn didn't rearrange them or move them to get a book?"

"I feel it." Her gaze darted around the room, alighting on cushions tucked into the corners of the couch, a blank pad of paper next to Quinn's landline phone, the corner of the throw rug in front of the mantel turned back—slight differences around the room that made the hair on the back of her neck quiver.

"Let me check the sliding back door." He strode toward Quinn's little dining area and checked the handle and the track of the door where Quinn had an extra lock inserted. "Both in place, just like I left them."

He yanked open the slider, and a cloud of salty sea air wafted into the room. "Remember, I checked all the doors and windows the night Quinn died. There was no sign of any break-in, Kyra."

"I know that. I remember." Clasping her hands in front of her, she did a turn in place. "I can't put my finger on it. The room feels different… ruffled."

Planting his hands on the kitchen table, Jake hunched forward. "Different from usual or different from the last time you were here…when we found Quinn?"

"That's it." She folded her arms and hunched her shoulders. "At first, I thought someone had broken in and killed Quinn."

Jake's mouth dropped open, and she continued to talk over him. "But now that I'm looking around, the differences I'm noticing are since our previous visit when we discovered Quinn's body."

"You think someone broke into Quinn's house and ruffled a few items after he died? Have you checked to see if anything has been stolen? Could be a tweaker or something, knowing the house is empty." Jake walked back into the living room and stood before the fireplace, his arms crossed, his feet planted on the rug.

"He has a safe in his bedroom closet. You wanted to look at that anyway, right? You told me Quinn had left you some weapons. Those would be in that safe."

"Do you have the combination with you?"

Kyra patted her purse. "I brought some of that info with me—including what should be in the safe. I think two of the guns he left to you are in there."

"I know he has a Makarov 9mm in there, a classic, and a German Luger." Jake peered around the room. "You don't see anything missing? Where's Quinn's computer?"

"He always used a desktop computer because he liked the monitor size, and he kept that in his office. This house has three bedrooms and two bathrooms. Besides his bedroom, one he kept as a guest room, and he turned the other into an office." She crooked her finger at Jake. "This way."

Her breathing had returned to normal once she realized she hadn't felt this disruption in Quinn's house the night he died, but only now. Of course, that night had been a whirlwind of emotions, and maybe she hadn't been attuned to the changes.

Jake followed her down the hallway, and she ducked into the first bedroom on the left. Quinn's computer sat on a desk with some sticky notes fluttering off the edges of the monitor and some bits of paper dotting the surface area of the desk.

Shuffling the mouse to wake up the computer, she said, "I know he didn't have this password-protected."

When the monitor came to life, Jake jabbed a finger at the tabs at the top of the browser. "Looks like Quinn was on Websleuths, the true crime site where The Player met his minions, and Sean Hughes's true crime blog, *LA Confidential*. He was following along with the investigation more than we thought."

"More than *you* thought." She clicked on the *LA Confidential* blog, which displayed the article where Hughes had outed her as the daughter of one of The Player's victims and detailed her troubled past as the killer of one of her foster fathers—in self-defense. Hughes had also functioned as the conduit between Jake and the third copycat, and had been murdered for his trouble.

She closed the browser and all the tabs with a click of the mouse. "We know his computer wasn't stolen. Doesn't mean someone didn't look at his files. Like I said, no password."

"Safe?" Jake jerked his thumb over his shoulder.

Kyra brushed past him and led him to the master bedroom, where Quinn had still slept in the king-size bed he'd shared with Charlotte. He'd admitted to Kyra once that he still left room for his wife on the left side, as if he expected her to be there one morning.

Blinking back tears, Kyra flicked the light switch on the outside of the walk-in closet and yanked open the door. Quinn had left one whole side of this closet empty, too, after Kyra had helped him pack up Charlotte's clothes. Now she'd have to do the same for his.

"The safe's in the corner, bolted to the floor." She fished a piece of paper from the purse strapped across her body. "I have the combination."

Jake held out his hand. "Let me."

"Are you afraid something's going to jump out at me?" She held on to the paper for a second before slapping it into his palm. "Go for it."

Jake crouched before the safe with the combination in one hand. He read out the numbers as he punched them into the keypad. A little scale of notes trilled, and a small display flashed green.

"Just like a hotel safe." As Jake paused, she nudged him in the back with her knee. "You *are* nervous about opening the safe."

"Just hoping those pieces are still in here." He

pulled open the door of the safe and plunged his hand inside. "Guns, cash and a few envelopes. Do you want me to take it all out?"

"Yes, please. I'm guessing one of those envelopes has info about his living trust and Terrence's phone number." She backed out of the closet. "Bring it out to the bed."

Jake emerged from the closet clutching several items to his chest with one arm, his other arm at his side with an old-fashioned-looking gun dangling from his fingertips. "The man was true to his word."

"Those are the weapons you expected to see in there?"

"They are." He dropped the contents of Quinn's safe on the neatly made-up bed and ran his hand along the barrel of one of the guns. "This piece is worth a lot of money. If you'd rather sell it and take the money, that's okay."

"That is most definitely *not* okay. Quinn cherished those guns, and that's why he wanted you to have them." She pushed three bundles of bills to the side and picked up one of the envelopes. She peeked inside, thumbing through some papers. "As I expected—instructions for his trust and Terrence's business card, which Quinn had given me some time ago."

"And the other envelope?" Jake made a grab for the envelope as she reached for it. He eyed the contents and let out a long breath. "Banking information, which I'm sure Hicks already has."

Kyra consulted a sheet of paper she'd pulled out of her purse. "Guns and cash. That's what he indicated, so it's all here."

"Nothing's been stolen from the house." Jake lifted his shoulders. "I think you're being fanciful about the idea that someone's been here. It's your mind playing tricks on you because Quinn's gone."

She sucked in her lower lip, and Jake dropped the gun he'd been caressing to the bed and took her in his arms. "Are you sure this isn't too soon for you? Let's grab Quinn's suit and get out of here for now. I can pour you a glass of wine and give you a nice massage."

Curling her arms around his neck, she planted a kiss on his mouth. "I'm so glad you're with me. Heart disease or no heart disease, I don't think Quinn could've ever left me unless he felt sure someone could protect me and make me happy— someone like you."

Jake ran a hand through the loose strands of her hair. "Quinn has nothing to worry about. I'm right by your side."

His warmth enveloped her, and she murmured against his solid chest. "So, Quinn didn't leave you instructions for my care and feeding? You're doing it of your own free will?"

Jake's frame stiffened in her arms, and she poked his side. "He *did* leave you instructions."

He backed out of her embrace and pinched her chin. "Don't be ridiculous. I told you. He left me descriptions of the two guns he wanted me to have. He already knew I'd be here to love and protect you."

"How'd I get so lucky?" She plucked at his shirt. "I'm going to dive back into the closet and collect Quinn's good suit. We can come back later to clean house. I—I may need some time before I can get to that."

"Take all the time you need, babe." He hoisted his two new pieces. "I'll put these back in the safe. What do you want to do with the cash? Looks like there's a bundle, couple grand at least."

"You can put that back, too. I'm thinking of giving it to that boxing gym here in Venice. Quinn had mentored a few of those young men who worked out there a couple of years ago." She wiped her nose with the back of her hand. "I think he'd like that."

"I think so, too." Jake flicked on the light to the walk-in closet and carried the guns and the cash to the back.

As he crouched in front of the safe, Kyra bumped him with her knees. "Sorry. I'm trying to get around you to the blue suit in the plastic. Thank goodness he had that dry-cleaned recently.

I believe the last time he wore it was for the funeral of that officer who was ambushed in Crenshaw. He probably never imagined his next time would be for his own funeral."

"Quinn always paid his respects. There will be a huge turnout for his funeral." Still on his haunches, Jake shifted out of her way and then stood up. "This closet's too small for the both of us. You get the suit and I'll lock up the windows and doors I opened."

As Jake slipped out of the closet, the empty hangers on Charlotte's side of the closet clacked and swayed, and the cellophane plastic protecting Quinn's suit whispered between her fingertips. Kyra swallowed and lifted the hanger from the rod. She carried the suit from the closet and laid it across the bed. Then she dipped back into the closet to look for a shirt, tie and shoes.

While she packed up the items on the bed, Jake appeared in the doorway of the bedroom. "The house is locked up. Do you want some help with that?"

"Yes, please." Kyra zipped up the garment bag and hoisted a small overnight suitcase over her shoulder. "I suppose I bring this stuff to the mortuary. I don't even have a mortuary."

Covering her face with her hands, she sank to the edge of the bed. "I don't know what I'm going to do."

The bed dipped as Jake sat beside her and draped an arm over her shoulder. "You do know what to do. You're doing it. You move ahead and think about and grieve for Quinn while you're doing it."

With Jake's help, she made it out of the house in one piece. As she walked past Quinn's neighbors, who had a gathering of friends in their front yard, one of the guys raised his beer and called out. "To Quinn."

The rest followed his lead, and Quinn's name echoed along the canal.

Kyra raised her hand. The night of Quinn's death, she'd resisted the urge to question his neighbors. The scene hadn't looked suspicious to the responding officers, nor to Jake, so they didn't canvass the neighborhood asking questions. The neighbors had known that Quinn passed, so if they'd had anything to report, they would've done so…right?

By the time they reached her apartment just about five miles away from Quinn's house, a lethargy had seeped into Kyra's bones. She could barely brush her teeth and pull the covers back on her bed.

As she drifted off, she could hear Jake putting away Quinn's things in her spare bedroom, taking out the trash and feeding Spot.

Kyra snuggled into her pillow, her eyes heavy.

Jake hovered over her, his breath warm on her cheek, and she felt a stab of guilt that she didn't want to make love. Maybe Jake thought she needed that closeness right now. Maybe she did.

She rolled onto her back and reached for him. "Coming to bed?"

"You looked so peaceful, I was going to let you sleep and then sneak out."

Her lashes fluttered, and she saw that he was still fully dressed. "I didn't mean to shut you out. You can spend the night. I thought you would."

"It's not that late, and I don't have any work clothes here." He brushed the hair from her eyes. "But I'll stay if you want me to."

"You're right." She aimed a blurry-eyed squint at her digital alarm clock on her nightstand. "It's not late at all—just feels like it. You can leave. Then you can go straight to work in the morning. I'll be okay."

"Are you sure?"

"I'm half asleep anyway." She cupped his strong jaw with her hand. "I'll see you tomorrow. Thanks for everything."

He kissed her hungrily. "Everything's locked up. Security systems are on."

"I'm fine. I'll see you tomorrow."

He kissed her again and then slipped from her room like a thief in the night. The best kind of thief, as he'd completely stolen her heart.

JAKE GOT BEHIND the wheel of his car and tossed Quinn's key chain in the cup holder. Quinn didn't want Kyra to know about the second bequest, and that involved a little subterfuge. Kyra's mood had made things a little easier for him. He'd have a hard time making love to Kyra knowing he planned to sneak to Quinn's behind her back.

He'd plotted ahead—leaving the safe in the closet unlocked to give himself an excuse to go back. But he hadn't needed it. The events of the past few days had drained Kyra. His poor baby couldn't even keep her eyes open.

Jake took the route down Lincoln back to Quinn's house. He parked on the street and launched into Quinn's neighborhood on the Venice canals. He crossed the water lilting against its manmade barrier as the wooden bridge huffed and wheezed. Quinn's rowdy neighbors had called it a night. Kyra had told him the guy next to Quinn was the drummer from an '80s rock band that still did reunion tours. Nice work if you could get it.

Jake reached Quinn's red door and used the key to let himself in. He turned on a lamp and studied the neat room. Had Kyra's sensitivity played tricks with her mind, or had someone really gotten in here after Quinn's death for a search? What could they be searching for? Kyra had already confirmed nothing of value was missing, although a former homicide detective like Quinn could possess many more valuables than cash, jewelry and electronics—and Jake was about to uncover one of those items.

He withdrew Quinn's map from his pocket and shook it out. The old detective must've gotten a little melodramatic in his old age, as he probably could've described the location of the floorboard with words just as well as pictures.

Kneeling by the fireplace, Jake flipped back the throw rug, which looked an awful lot like those pillows Kyra had on her couch. He checked the map in the light from his cell phone and counted the floorboards from the edge of the fireplace.

He pressed on the edges of the wood slats until he felt a rim, and then pulled a knife from his pocket. He slid the blade along the edges and lifted.

About ten minutes later, he had a pile of wood pieces at his elbow and a gaping hole in the floor. His nose twitched as he aimed his light into the crevasse, the odor of brine strong. Something gleamed when the beam of his light hit it. He reached in with one hand and curled his fingers around the hard edge of a metal box.

With cobwebs clinging to his hand, he pulled it out. He balanced the slim container on his palms and blew dust from its surface. He sneezed. If someone *had* gotten into Quinn's house, he or she hadn't gotten this far.

Clutching the metal container, Jake backed up to Quinn's recliner. He sank into the chair and turned on the lamp next to it.

The container looked like something you might use for classified documents. It had an actual locking device on it, but Quinn had provided Jake with the combination, just as he'd left the combination to the safe in the closet for Kyra.

Jake held the piece of paper beneath the yellow glow of the lamp and memorized the numbers. His fingers played across the surface of the lockbox, entering the combination.

When it clicked, he hesitated. Holding his breath, he opened the lid on the box. His gaze alighted on a plain manila envelope with no label on the outside.

He used his fingernails to bend the clasp, still firm, still in place. He lifted the flap and pulled out a sheaf of papers. His eyebrows collided over his nose.

He held in his hands a crime scene report, yellowed at the corners. It resembled the ones the LAPD used today with a few alterations.

His pulse jumped when he read the date and location at the top of the page. Why did Quinn have a copy of the crime scene report of Jennifer Lake's murder holed up in his floor?

He flipped through the pages at the top. He'd read the report of Kyra's mother's murder many times before. So many times, in fact, he practically had it memorized—that's how he spotted some minor differences. Time, body condition and location were all the same, but there were slight changes from the original. Or was this the original?

He continued shuffling through the pages until he got to the end with a description of the child, Kyra, at the scene. Jake skimmed down that page and then sat up, his heart beating erratically in his chest.

He'd just spotted a huge difference from the original report. The child, Marilyn Lake, had not been in the bedroom when the officer, patrolman Carlos Castillo, arrived. She'd been sitting beside the dead body of her mother, the phone from the 911 call still clutched in her hand.

Furthermore, the child hadn't been asleep in her bed when The Player had killed her mother. She'd been peering at him from a crack in her bedroom door.

Kyra Chase had witnessed her mother's murder. She'd seen The Player with her own two eyes.

# Chapter Six

A day later Jake stared at the stills from the condo's security cameras with unseeing eyes.

Kyra witnessed her mother's murder. She'd seen The Player. Quinn knew all along. The words kept thrumming through his head on a nonstop loop.

Did Kyra remember? No. That's why Quinn had hidden the file under his floorboards. She didn't remember what she saw as a child, and Quinn never told her she'd been a witness. Quinn never told anyone. The department never knew, the press never knew and The Player himself never knew. Or did he?

Jake ran a hand across his mouth. Was that why The Player had kept tabs on Kyra all these years? He knew he'd left a witness and had been waiting for the other shoe to drop. But it never had. Did he realize why his secret had been safe with Kyra? Did he know Quinn had done everything in his power to protect that eight-year-old girl, even if it meant ignoring an important lead?

Quinn hadn't included a description of the killer in that initial report. Maybe Kyra told him nothing more than that the killer had been a man. She'd been a traumatized child and clearly she'd forgotten whatever it was she saw.

Jake's gaze wandered from his computer screen to the back of Kyra's head as she sat at her desk across the room, her blond ponytail swaying slightly as she typed on her keyboard. Quinn hadn't wanted Kyra to know, hadn't wanted her to remember, but Jake didn't play those games. He was honest, almost to a fault. How could he keep this from Kyra?

He bit the inside of his cheek so hard, he tasted the metallic flavor of blood on his tongue. How would it help her to know? How would it help the case? She didn't remember that she'd seen The Player—Quinn had made sure of that—and she wouldn't remember now.

There had actually been a conspiracy of silence between Quinn and Castillo.

Castillo had been the responding officer the night of Jennifer Lake's murder. He had to have known Jennifer's daughter saw the killer. But Castillo had kept quiet, too. Why?

Falsifying a report like that could mean big trouble, but Quinn and Castillo had kept this pact for twenty years. Why would Castillo jeopardize his career like that? Quinn did it for Kyra, and he could've retired at any time if the brass found out what he did. Quinn didn't care, but Castillo's career was on the upswing.

Jake drummed his thumbs against the keyboard. In fact, Castillo's career took a steep trajectory upward around the time of The Player homicides. Quinn had added the young patrolman to the task force, and Castillo had made a name for himself.

Was that the payoff? Silence for a career boost?

He blinked, and it took him a few second to realize Kyra had twisted around in her chair and was trying to catch his attention. He lifted his eyebrows, and she tapped her phone.

He swiped his personal cell from his desk and read Kyra's text inviting him to lunch. He hadn't talked to her all morning. He'd been true to his word last night and headed home after digging up his final bequest from Quinn. The report now was nestled securely in his own home safe.

He responded in the affirmative to Kyra's lunch invite and returned to the video from Erica's condo, showing her killer skulking down her hallway minutes before he forced his way into her place to murder her—thinking she was the witness in the Angeles National Forest.

A ripple of fear coursed down his spine. Had

The Player instructed his minions to kill any witnesses because he had left one himself twenty
years ago?

Leaning forward, he studied the hunched-
over form, obscuring the killer's real height. The
baggy hoodie concealed his body type, and the
hat pulled low over his forehead hid his face. This
guy could be a hundred men walking the streets
of LA right now. Eyewitness accounts provided
some of the weakest evidence for a case. Show
five different people the same scene and ask them
to recount it later, and those five people were very
likely to give you five different accounts.

"How long are you going to stare at that,
brother?" Billy clapped him on the shoulder.
"Nothing to see."

"Did you catch him leaving, by any chance?"

"As we suspected, he left through an unmonitored back door. He could've headed out to a car
anywhere along there. No luck."

Jake pushed away from his desk and crossed
his hands behind his head. "The sheriff's department doesn't have much evidence from inside the
condo, either. He must've been wearing gloves,
no prints anywhere. They're looking for hair, fibers, but with no suspect, those could belong to
anyone. There is a partial shoe print where he
kicked open the door, but it's a common sneaker,

and we can't tell the size because we don't have the whole sole of the shoe."

Billy held up a finger. "One piece of good news, if you want to call it that. We got a call today about a young woman missing for a couple of days. Could be our victim. Description matches."

"I have lunch in a minute." Jake shut down the video on his laptop. "Do you want me to stick around for the ID instead?"

"No, I got it covered. The missing woman's brother is coming in. I'll let you know either way." Billy plucked his cell phone from his pocket and paused. "I heard our man Quinn left you a couple of sweet pieces."

"Word gets around, doesn't it?" Jake grabbed his jacket from the back of his chair. "Yeah, Quinn left me some…interesting stuff."

Kyra had left the war room before him. It was a game they played to keep their interactions at the station professional, even though everyone knew they were in a relationship and often had lunch together. As Jake reached the door, he almost bumped into Captain Castillo charging into the room.

Holding up his hands, Jake said, "Whoa, excuse me, Captain. You in a hurry?"

"I was on my way to speak to Billy about the possible ID on the vic."

"He just told me. I hope we can give that poor girl on the slab a name." As he squeezed past Castillo, the captain touched his arm.

"Did you and Kyra have a chance to go out to Quinn's to look for the items he left you?"

Jake's expression froze in place. Without a flick of his eye, he said, "I looked at the weapons he left me and decided to keep them in his safe for now, and Kyra picked out a suit for the burial. We'll be back to clean up."

Castillo skimmed a hand through his salt-and-pepper hair. "You might need some help. Quinn has a lot of stuff in that house."

"Have you been there recently?"

"N-no, not recently, not for several months."

"It's not too bad. I can help Kyra get the house in shape, whether she wants to keep it, sell it or live in it. We'll go through everything."

Jake stayed just long enough to see Castillo's face pale under his brown skin. He wanted to talk over this development with Kyra, but like Castillo, he was keeping a secret. Damn, he hated secrets.

As he exited the station, Kyra caught up with him, nudging him in the back with her purse. "Wait up."

He pretended to stumble and grabbed her arm. "I thought you didn't want to be seen with me at the station."

"We're coworkers having lunch. That's allowed, isn't it?" She tried to shake him off, but he tightened his grip.

"So is this." He leaned over and kissed her on her blushing cheek. "It's not like I'm your boss or you're mine. Hell, you don't even technically work for the LAPD. You're a contractor, and we're paying you for your service. Besides, it's too late for decorum now."

"Because everyone knows we're an item." She squeezed his hand before jerking free. "Doesn't mean we have to feed the rumor mill."

He stabbed at his remote and unlocked the car. Then he beat Kyra to the passenger side and opened her door. "I like the sound of that—feeding the rumor mill. What would we have to do to get that going?"

"Don't—" she flattened her hand against his belly as she slid into the car "—even think about it."

Jake practically jogged to the driver's side. Kyra's mood seemed to be lifting. The visit to Quinn's last night had been tough for her to bear. How much tougher would it have been had she discovered she'd witnessed her mother's murder and Quinn had been hiding it from her all these years?

He couldn't tell her just yet. He'd been thinking about breaking it to her over bowls of steaming pho, but he didn't want to bring her down. Right now, he was more interested in finding out why Castillo had kept Quinn's secret. They'd both colluded in changing a police report for a murder scene.

Fifteen minutes later, they were sitting across from each other at a small table crowded with their drinks and a tray filled with cilantro, jalapeños, bean sprouts and a variety of other condiments to enhance their pho.

Kyra planted her elbows on the table and twirled the straw in her drink. "You seem preoccupied. Did you get anything more out of that video?"

"His hoodie, hat and baggy clothes hid his identity well. He left via an unmonitored back door, so we have no footage at the front of the building." He spread his hands on the table. "Not much to go on, but Billy may be identifying the victim today."

"That should help. Gives you another crime scene if you know where he abducted her." She took a sip of her drink. "Something else?"

He couldn't discuss his suspicions about Castillo with her without telling her the truth about the night her mother died—and he wasn't ready to do that yet.

He shrugged. "Wondering when this is going to end. I want Fiona down here for Christmas, but not if I'm still working this case or, God help us, another copycat killer case."

She covered his hand, curled into a tight ball on the table. "You know when this is going to end. It's going to end when you stop The Player."

"I'm afraid you're right. How can we catch The Player?" He shoved a hand into his hair. "Maybe Quinn and I will be alike in more ways than I want to count. Maybe The Player will outplay both of us."

"He's shown himself." She stopped as the waitress appeared with two bowls of pho, steam curling from the surface. When the server left, Kyra continued. "You have tools at your disposal that Quinn could only dream of twenty years ago. He had faith in you…and so do I. You can do this, Jake, you and Billy and the whole task force."

"Damn, I miss Quinn." He sniffed, and it wasn't because he'd just dumped some jalapeño in his soup. "He was my sounding board. He was my friend."

Kyra smoothed the pad of her thumb along the inside of his wrist. "He felt the same way about you."

Jake blinked and sipped from his spoon, his nose tingling. That was the pho—maybe. "I didn't see you earlier in the morning. Were you able to get Quinn's suit to the funeral home?"

"Not yet, but I did get the name of the mortuary from Terrence." She sprinkled some cilantro on top of her soup and glanced up. "The coroner hasn't released Quinn, umm, Quinn's body yet. Is that normal?"

"Haven't heard from him yet—I mean, her. Dr. Ellis is doing the autopsy. Her husband is a cop, and I know she'll take special care to do a thorough job."

"That's good to hear." She plunged her spoon into her pho. "Hey, I meant to ask you. You did take the keys to Quinn's house, didn't you? Tell me you did."

He gulped the spicy soup too fast and choked. "I discovered this morning that I had them in my pocket. I probably forgot to give them back to you after I locked up last night."

"Okay, that's a relief. I thought I lost them. I mean, I still have my own key to the house, but I wouldn't want to lose Quinn's set."

He asked, "Are you still convinced someone broke into Quinn's place after he was killed to search it?"

"Convinced?" She waved her hand in front of her puckered lips and took a sip of her drink. "As we didn't notice anything missing, I'm not so sure. But I swear, certain items seemed...placed, as if someone wanted to put everything back just as he'd found it."

Jake jerked his head. "Did Castillo have a key to Quinn's place?"

"Captain Castillo?" Kyra narrowed her eyes. "Why would you ask that? What would the captain want from Quinn's house?"

Jake shoved a spoonful of soup, chock-full of veggies and chicken, into his mouth to give himself time to think. Just because the thought came to him in a flash, he didn't have to give voice to it.

"Not that he'd want anything—" besides the police report he and Quinn had eighty-sixed in favor of a revised version "—but maybe he went in there to pay his respects, look around. You said yourself, nothing was missing."

"That's a thought. I'm not sure if Captain Castillo had a key, though. Not sure why he would."

Because they were partners in a cover-up.

"Just thinking outside the box." Jake swiped a napkin across his mouth. "Speaking of thinking outside the box, do you think it would be worth it to hypnotize Piper?"

Kyra dropped her spoon. "Hypnotize her? You mean to see if she remembers anything more about the killer?"

"Do you believe in that sort of thing?"

"I absolutely do, and I think we have one of the best hypnotherapists in the business right here in LA. I'm not sure it would help Piper, though. It's not like she can't remember him. She does, but she saw him in the dark at a distance, and he was wearing a hoodie and a hat—just like when he killed Erica. I don't believe a hypnotherapist could get anything else out of her. She hasn't buried the memory. She just didn't get a good look at him." She gave him a thumbs-up. "I'm impressed. You've come a long way, from a guy who didn't trust therapists several months ago to someone who's suggesting hypnosis for a witness."

"Why wouldn't I? I've been schooled by the best." He dabbed at several cilantro leaves on the table and crushed them between his fingers. "But you do believe hypnosis can uncover blocked memories."

"I do. I've seen it work. Why? Do you have some memories you want unlocked?" She winked at him.

"Me? I have a few I'd rather forget." Pushing his bowl away, he changed the subject. "Fiona wants to know if she can do a video chat with you later. She wants to interview you about your job for a class assignment."

Kyra turned pink. She and his daughter had gotten off to a rocky start, probably because they were too similar, but ever since Kyra risked her life to save Fiona's, his daughter had become Kyra's biggest fan—next to him.

"Have her text me. I'd be more than happy to help out."

"At least she doesn't want to interview me. I couldn't tell her half the stuff I do." He held up his cup and shook it, rattling the ice. "Do you want a refill before we head back? I haven't heard from Cool Breeze, so I don't think they ID'd the victim yet. He probably needs my help."

"I'll tell him you said that." She handed him her cup. "Diet, lots of ice."

When he got back to the table after topping up their drinks, Kyra shoved his phone at him. "Can you call Dr. Ellis before we leave and ask about Quinn's autopsy, please?"

"I'll do it in the car. That way, I can put it on speaker so you can hear."

They grabbed their drinks and headed back to the car. Once inside, Jake pulled out his phone. He scrolled through his contacts and placed a call to the coroner's office.

Someone at the front desk of the ME's office picked up on the second ring, and Jake put his phone on speaker for Kyra. "This is Detective Jake McAllister. I'm calling for Dr. Ellis regarding an autopsy."

"Oh, Detective McAllister, Dr. Ellis has a note to call you. I'm looking at it right here. She had a meeting, but I think they just broke up. I'll let her know you're on the phone."

"Thanks." Jake nodded at Kyra and said, "She's probably done. You can let Terrence know."

A woman's breathless voice came over the line. "Jake? I'm glad you called. Your ears must've been burning, as I was going to call you right after my meeting."

"Perfect, Deirdre. Are you finished with Quinn's autopsy? We have a big funeral to plan."

Deirdre paused. "Uh, not so fast, Jake."

Jake's heart skipped a beat. Licking his lips, he shot a glance at Kyra. Maybe putting the doc on speaker wasn't the best idea.

"Does that mean you're not finished?"

"I have to do some toxicology follow-up, and that could take a few days." He heard some papers shuffling across the line, and then Deirdre cleared her throat. "I found a needle puncture on Quinn's body."

Kyra's hand had been creeping toward his leg, and now she grabbed his thigh.

Jake's nostrils flared with a snort. "Are you suggesting Quinn was using drugs?"

"No evidence of that. One pinprick between his first and second toe on his left foot." Deirdre paused again, this one causing the hair on Quinn's arms to stand on end.

"What are you saying, Deirdre?"

"I'm suggesting Detective Roger Quinn may have been murdered."

# *Chapter Seven*

Kyra dug her fingernails into Jake's leg. The sound of Dr. Ellis's words still echoed in the car. She wanted to scream. She wanted to punch the dashboard. She wanted to know more.

"I can't tell you much other than that right now, Jake."

Kyra tugged on Jake's sleeve. She didn't want to say anything that might get him in trouble for allowing her to listen in, so she kept silent, but Dr. Ellis had to spill more details after making that shocking pronouncement.

Jake dipped his chin to his chest. "You can tell me what led you to that suspicion, Deirdre. You have to give me more than that."

She sighed but delivered. "When I started Quinn's examination, I vowed to do my very best for him. Sure, I had his medical records and knew about the heart disease, saw the stents for myself, but those stents were doing their job. His arteries were clear enough that if he'd had an angiograph the day he died, it wouldn't have shown enough closure for another stent or bypass surgery. He was managing, so I looked elsewhere. I'd noticed two things when we removed his clothing—his right shoe was tied differently from his left and his right sock was on inside-out. Would I have bothered with those details if I'd seen atherosclerosis in his arteries? Nope. But it got me thinking. May have even learned a thing or two from you, J-Mac."

Kyra pressed a hand to her heart, which was in danger of galloping out of her chest. She knew it. Deep down she'd known it all along.

Dr. Ellis took a sip of something and continued. "So, I took a look at that foot, examined the area between the toes where addicts often shoot up—not that I believed for a minute Quinn was using. He didn't have any of the signs of addiction or habitual use. Lo and behold, I discovered a pinprick. Looked a helluva lot to me like a syringe. So I ordered another set of toxicology reports."

Jake asked, "What are you looking for, Deirdre?"

She clicked her tongue. "You know, Jake. I'm looking for a drug that can simulate a heart attack, some kind of stimulant."

Jake talked to the doctor for a few more minutes about timing and schedules, but the roaring in Kyra's ears had blocked their conversation.

As soon as Jake ended the call, Kyra turned to him and grabbed his arm. "I knew it. He killed him."

Jake sat with his head down, the phone cupped between his hands. "The Player? You think The Player killed Quinn?"

"Who else?" She rubbed her arms. "I just don't know how he could've gotten into Quinn's house. How did he manage to shoot him up between his toes?"

Lifting his head, Jake scratched his jaw. "You remember Quinn had the bump on the back of his head."

She froze, pressing her hands against her bouncing knees. "The first responders, and even you, figured he got that when he fell, hitting his head on the coffee table. He was in the right position for that."

"What if that was a setup? What if someone hit Quinn on the head to knock him out, and then pulled off his shoe and sock to shoot him up, put the shoe and sock back on—incorrectly—and then positioned him to make it look like the heart attack, which was induced, caused him to fall and hit his head?"

Kyra covered her mouth and she rocked forward.

"Death by heart attack instead of a fall because it would be expected, given his condition." Jake gripped the steering wheel, his knuckles white. "It's just speculation."

She shot back in her seat, adrenaline rushing through her body, the wheels in her brain clicking. "Damn good speculation, Detective. Quinn would be proud, but how?"

"How what?"

"Quinn never would've allowed a stranger into his house. Never would've turned his back on one."

"Maybe The Player is no stranger to Quinn."

"I don't even know what that means." Kyra massaged her temples, now throbbing. "You think Quinn knew who The Player was?"

"Listen." Jake squeezed the back her neck. "What if The Player is one of Quinn's acquaintances? This person comes to Quinn's house and Quinn lets him in because he knows him. Quinn turns his back on him, the guy hits him with something and then arranges the heart attack, never imagining a sharp ME like Dr. Ellis would think to look between his toes."

Kyra ground her teeth together, her jaw tight. "If it happened that way, I will never let this rest. I won't be satisfied until the man who murdered my mother *and* my father is brought to justice."

As SOON AS they got back to the station, Billy swooped in on Jake and carried him away. An hour later, they made public the name of the first victim of the fourth copycat killer.

Ashley Russell had been a young woman struggling to make it in LA. Her brother had told Billy that she'd been attending AA meetings, and had been at one the evening she disappeared. The task force would send someone to question people at the AA meeting, but they probably wouldn't get too far with the people there who wanted to maintain their anonymity and the anonymity of others.

Kyra glanced around the room and shut down her laptop. The team would give her more information on Ashley and her family and friends tomorrow. She had a brother in the picture, so Kyra would most likely start with him if he requested assistance. Nobody would miss her now, and her only patient of the afternoon had canceled.

She had a little of her own detective work to do. Neither Dr. Ellis nor Jake would be releasing any news about Quinn's autopsy until the ME office completed it and the second set of toxicology tests came back. That gave her time to do some amateur sleuthing.

She slipped out of the war room without a second glance and drove straight to Quinn's house in Venice. Quinn didn't have security cameras at his house. Venice contained several dodgy areas, but the neighborhood in the canals wasn't among them. Thieves would have to lug anything they stole out of the neighborhood on foot, which must be a deterrent.

Quinn's car still claimed his parking spot outside of the canals, so Kyra parked along the street. She always kept her key to Quinn's house on her key chain, but now she had Quinn's key chain, as well—the one Jake had forgotten to leave at her place last night.

She pulled it from her purse now, and gripped it in her hand as she crossed the bridge to his house. She let herself in and stood on the threshold for a minute, surveying the room. It *did* have an air of being tidied. She hadn't imagined that last night, and Dr. Ellis's bombshell today gave her more proof.

Perhaps the killer himself had returned to the scene of his crime to gather evidence or make sure he hadn't left anything behind. If he were a friend of Quinn's, he could explain his presence if caught.

She released the breath she'd been holding and stepped into the room, leaving the door open behind her. If Quinn's toxicology results came back positive for some type of amphetamine in his system and his death was declared a homicide, the CSIs would descend on this house with a fury. But what would they find?

Quinn's prints, hers and Jake's would be all over the place. If Clive Stewart, their fingerprint tech, picked up others, those people would have to provide alibis. There's no way Quinn's friend-turned-killer came in wearing gloves. Of course, he could've wiped his prints after the murder. Even though the end of fall was near, nobody was wearing gloves in LA at this time of the year.

She covered her mouth with one hand. How could The Player have befriended Quinn? Quinn didn't make friends easily, didn't socialize much and was highly suspicious of new acquaintances. That tiny speculation that The Player could be a cop tickled the edges of her mind. Was that what they were looking at?

She took a turn around the room, examining the areas that had caught her attention last night—the bookcase with the two pictures straightened instead of facing the room at an angle, the pillows on the couch neatly tucked into the corners instead of shoved against the back cushion, the throw rug...

She tripped to a stop. Last night, the corner of the rug had been turned back. Now it was straight. She or Jake must've flicked it into position.

She crouched beside the place where they'd discovered Quinn's body and peered at the corner of the coffee table. The EMTs had noted the fresh lump on the back of Quinn's head, and Jake and the other cops on the scene had assumed he'd hit it on his way down, collapsing from the heart attack.

Jake had even spotted a smear of blood on the wood, but that would be easy to arrange. From her position on the floor, Kyra tilted back her head, imagining the scene. Quinn had fallen a few steps from the kitchen. Had he and his guest gone into the kitchen for something to drink?

She and Jake had figured Quinn had been coming out of the kitchen with a glass of water in his hand. The glass hadn't broken when Quinn went down but had rolled onto the area rug in front of the fireplace, spilling its contents along the way.

But what if someone had gone into the kitchen with him? What if Quinn had been bringing that water for someone else? She'd always been after Quinn to drink more water. He didn't like it and preferred soda or iced tea. Maybe that water had been for someone else.

If his fake friend were behind Quinn, though, he might've had his own drink. They hadn't found a second glass, of course, but the killer could've left it on the counter while he went after Quinn to knock him down. Once he had him on the floor, unconscious or disoriented, he pulled off his shoe and sock and shot him up between the toes, never believing someone would be looking for needle marks on retired detective Roger Quinn.

Kyra sprang up from the floor and barreled into the kitchen. She'd left the glass Quinn dropped in the sink, and it still sat there, undisturbed. She yanked open the dishwasher. When Quinn ate alone, he preferred to wash his dishes by hand, and his dishwasher reflected this. A handful of utensils stuck up from the basket on the side, a few plates nestled neatly in a row and one glass commanded the entire top tray.

She eyed the glass. Could that be the one? She'd ask Jake to collect it as evidence and have Clive run it for prints. Quinn's should be the only prints on the glass. Would the killer be careless enough to leave a glass in the dishwasher?

She sidestepped to the cupboard where Quinn kept his dishes and pulled open the cabinet door. Similar glasses to the one in the sink and the dishwasher stood at attention in a row on the shelf. One stuck out from the others. Had the killer rinsed out his glass, dried it, wiped it clean and put it back in the cupboard? She'd mention this one to Jake, too.

If Quinn's death had been a murder, and she had to keep telling herself that wasn't a forgone conclusion yet, enough people had trudged through the crime scene to render it useless.

A light tap on the open front door had Kyra clutching her throat and spinning around.

"Kyra, is that you? It's Rose." Rose Bernstein,

one of Quinn's neighbors and friends, poked her fluffy blond head into the house.

Patting her chest, where her heart thumped back to normal, Kyra called out, "Yes, Rose. I'm in the kitchen."

She closed the cupboard and returned to the living room, where Rose had one tentative foot over the threshold.

"When I saw the open door, I was hoping it was you." Rose tugged her sweater around her thin frame, slightly stooped with osteoporosis. "May I?"

"Of course." She waved Rose into the room. "Come in."

Rose floated forward, stretching out her hands, the blue veins running crisscross on the backs under thin skin. "My dear girl, I'm so sorry for your loss."

Kyra met her halfway, and the older woman wrapped her in a hug, patting her back, enveloping her in a scent of faded lilacs. When Rose finally released her, Kyra had to grab a tissue from her purse. She'd never met any of her grandparents, but Rose smelled exactly how she'd always imagined a grandma to smell.

"Quinn was your friend, too. I know you're going to miss him."

"Who am I going to cook for now? My son and the grandkids live in New York." She shrugged a set of narrow shoulders. "But now I feel guilty about all those meals I sent to Quinn. He probably shouldn't have been eating lasagna with four different cheeses."

"He loved your cooking." Kyra squeezed her arm, sealing her own lips. It could be the lasagna had nothing to do with Quinn's death. "When was the last time you saw Quinn?"

Rose shook her head. "That's the sad thing. I had been away in Palm Springs, visiting my sister for a few days. I heard about his death from the neighbors when I got back. I wasn't even here. Didn't even see him before he died."

Kyra sucked in her bottom lip. No use asking Rose if she'd seen or heard anything unusual. She wouldn't bother questioning Quinn's nearest neighbor, the drummer next door. She'd leave that up to Jake or Billy once they started investigating Quinn's death as a homicide.

Had Quinn really known The Player all these years and not felt something from him? Some vibe? Some connection?

The Player obviously was very good at appearing human. He'd lived among normal people for years, maybe even had a wife and children. You always had to wonder if the families of serial killers were telling the truth when they proclaimed dear old dad was just like any other father on the block. The BTK killer had walked his daughter down the aisle.

A little shiver crept over Kyra's flesh, and she squared her shoulders, recalibrating. "I'm sorry you missed saying goodbye to Quinn, but none of us knew our last time was a goodbye. Do you want to have a seat? I was just going through Quinn's kitchen to…see what I could throw out."

"I can't stay long, but don't worry about that kitchen. I can clean it up for you. Unless you want any of the food, I can dispose of it and donate the nonperishables to a shelter I work with here in Venice." Rose dangled a single key from a ring. "Quinn and I had keys to each other's places. I can give it to you now, or I can hang on to it and see about that kitchen."

"You're so kind. That would be helpful, but can you hold off on doing anything in the kitchen until I tell you to move ahead?"

"Of course, whatever you need." Rose reached out and patted Kyra's hand. "I'm glad I saw you today. When I noticed the door open, I thought it might be you and I had missed you yesterday, and then you didn't come back with Jake—Detective McAllister."

"Come back?" Kyra tilted her head to the side. Had someone been in the house after she and Jake left last night? "We didn't come back. Did you see someone in the house?"

"I know you didn't come back, but your young man returned later."

Kyra's cheeks warmed at the thought of Jake being her *young man*, but Rose had it wrong and maybe she saw the killer. "Jake and I went back to my place, and then he went home. He didn't go to Quinn's house."

"Oh." Rose fluffed her perm. "Maybe he forgot something and didn't mention it to you, but it was definitely Jake I saw last night. Poco, my Chihuahua, had to take a potty break around midnight, so I walked him outside. I saw Jake coming across the bridge. I almost called out because I thought you might be with him, but he was alone."

"H-he went into the house?" And then Kyra remembered Jake handing over Quinn's key chain at lunch. He claimed he'd forgotten he had it in his pants pocket.

"He let himself into the house with a key and turned on a light in the living room." Rose knitted her eyebrows. "That's all right, isn't it? He was a friend of Quinn's. In fact, Quinn adored that man, and, well, he's a police officer."

Kyra blinked rapidly. "Of course it's okay. He probably stopped here on the way back to his place because he forgot something when we were here earlier."

"Well, I'm glad I got to see you." Rose made

a move for the front door. "Let me know when I can get into that kitchen. I want to help you in any way I can. Quinn would want that."

Kyra walked Rose to the door and watched the birdlike woman cross the wooden bridge to her own side of the neighborhood, her house across from Quinn's.

Even after Rose disappeared into her house with a wave, Kyra stayed on the porch, watching the seawater lap against the concrete barrier that formed the canal. Jake might have forgotten something at Quinn's earlier, but he had all that time during lunch to tell her and a perfect opportunity to mention it when he returned Quinn's key chain to her.

She clenched her teeth and stepped back inside her house, slamming the door behind her. Jake didn't tell her because he'd come sneaking back here on his own.

Because Jake had a secret.

# *Chapter Eight*

Captain Carlos Castillo had a secret, had kept it for twenty years.

Jake watched Castillo through narrowed eyes as the captain leaned over Billy's computer to study the stills of Erica's killer. Why had Castillo agreed to change that report? He'd put his career on the line by agreeing to appease Detective Roger Quinn.

Castillo's actions ever since the copycat killers had surfaced several months ago had been suspect. The captain had been jumpy, stressed out, overly curious about Jake's budding relationship with both Kyra and Quinn.

Had he been the one searching Quinn's place after the old detective's death? Had he been searching for that report to squelch it? Castillo had to know that Jake would have the same concerns about that report going public. Kyra's safety had to be Jake's priority, just as it had been Quinn's.

Had Castillo gone even further than breaking and entering? Had he gone to Quinn's that day demanding that he destroy the original report? When Quinn refused, had he hit him over the head? No. If Dr. Ellis was correct about the injection between Quinn's toes, his murder had been deliberate and planned—not a moment of fury.

That didn't mean Castillo and Quinn hadn't argued about this before. Castillo could've planned to take out Quinn once he realized the detective wouldn't come around to his way of thinking and destroy that report.

Why hadn't Quinn burned the original report? Maybe he knew deep down, as Jake did, that Kyra had a right to know the truth about the night of her mother's murder. She'd want to know.

"Something to add, J-Mac?" Castillo must've felt Jake's stare and now met Jake's eyes with his own, dark and unfathomable.

Jake twitched his head. "Just wondering if you guys had any luck with the zooming, but it doesn't sound like it."

"This guy—" Billy flicked his finger at the screen "—looks like thousands of other white guys in LA. He's too smart to smile at the camera."

"Not too smart to go after a witness and then wind up killing the wrong person." Jake glanced up at the door of the war room for the hundredth time that morning.

Kyra had gone off and done her own thing yesterday afternoon when they'd been scrambling to notify Ashley's family and questioning her brother. She'd sent him a terse text last night and hadn't answered his texts so far today. He hoped Quinn's death wasn't hitting her particularly hard right now, especially as that death might be a murder.

Billy replied, "He didn't want to violate one of The Player's rules—don't leave any witnesses—but he went overboard. Maybe he'll stop at Ashley, seeing how he messed up so much."

"Let's hope so." Castillo rapped his knuckles on the desk and made a quick exit.

Jake drilled the captain's back with his gaze as he left the room. Castillo had gotten that sheen on his forehead when Billy had mentioned witnesses. If Jake wanted the whole story about Jennifer Lake's murder, he had to confront Castillo. But first, he needed some proof or at least some ammunition.

He ducked his head and tapped the keyboard to bring up the personnel database. He didn't have access to go into anyone's individual files, but he could view their progress through the LAPD—time on the job, promotions, accolades, that kind of thing.

He clicked on the link for the Northeast Division, where Castillo had spent his entire career.

After looking left and right, Jake pulled the laptop closer to him and scrolled down the alphabet to find Castillo's name. He selected it.

Captain Carlos Castillo's glorious career with the LAPD tumbled down the screen. Jake scanned the very beginning of Castillo's positions, and then zeroed in on the few years The Player was active.

Castillo had been working patrol during that time, and that's why he'd been the first to respond to a child's 911 call that her mother was dead. The year before that, Castillo had supported a drug task force. Jake hunched forward, clicking through the cases that the task force had solved.

He'd read about this before. Armando Sandoval, a drug kingpin from the Sinaloa cartel, had controlled the streets of LA during this period, and the LAPD had formed a task force, LA Impact, to bring him down. The team had been mostly successful, reeling in the small fish first, the pushers on the corners and in the playgrounds. They'd squealed on the bigger fish and so on and so on, until the task force reached Sandoval, the big whale—or shark would be a better term. The DEA had ended up killing Sandoval in a gun battle at the border, but LA Impact had had a hand in the confrontation.

He scrolled through some of the cases, and his hand jerked when Quinn's name popped up. He'd been investigating the murder of a young woman who'd been shot in her car while her son wailed in his car seat in the back. Quinn had discovered that the woman's boyfriend, and the father of her baby, was one of Sandoval's dealers.

Jake drilled down further into the report. Tony Galecki had graduated from selling on the corner to distributing and managing a team of dealers. But something had gone wrong. Tony double-crossed the cartel by cutting the original product, selling more of it and pocketing what he thought the cartel would never notice. He was wrong. The cartel noticed everything. Tony's girlfriend paid the price.

The report didn't end with the girlfriend's death and Tony's arrest, though. The stacks of cash Tony had accumulated had gone missing. Looked like Internal Affairs had been called in for a hot minute, but the issue had been resolved. Tony had recanted his story about the missing money, and the investigation went away.

Jake dug some more, and his fingertips buzzed. Much of IA's suspicions had been directed at Carlos Castillo. He'd done a search of Tony's place, including a storage unit. He found packets of the diluted product but never found Tony's money.

Jake's heart skipped a beat when he saw some of the personal evidence IA had started to investigate about the hotshot patrolman. Castillo had been going through a divorce at the time. Jake had seen the happy family pictures in Castillo's office, which had come after the first marriage. Divorces were expensive—he knew all about that even though he'd gotten off easily. Tess had just wanted their marriage over so she could start again with Brock. His ex had gotten a friend of hers from law school to handle their divorce and it had been as painless and inexpensive as possible. But Jake realized what it could've been— something more like Castillo's.

IA was about to look into some of Castillo's finances at the time, but that ended when Tony admitted he'd lied about the money being missing. Claimed he and his girlfriend had already spent most of it or had given it away.

Steepling his fingers, Jake minimized the screen and leaned back in his chair. Quinn had been involved in a murder case that had found its way onto the LA Impact task force, a task force that Castillo had worked. This had occurred just prior to the formation of The Player task force.

Jake drummed his fingers on the desk. What had happened to Tony Galecki's money? The cartels didn't tolerate lying or stealing, ironically enough, but the sums had to be high for them to take out a woman with her baby. Had Tony and his girlfriend been able to spend that much and that fast? Why had Tony changed his mind at the last minute?

He planned to find out.

He jumped when Billy nudged his arm. "Earth to Jake. Are you down for some lunch?"

"Lunch already?" Jake rubbed his eyes. "That went fast."

"Did you find anything worth reporting?" Billy jabbed his finger at Jake's laptop, the LAPD screensaver innocuously bouncing from one edge to the other.

"Nah. You?"

"Nothing on the videos, nothing at the crime scene in the Angeles National Forest. Copycat Four must've followed The Player's other rules, even though he messed up the witness one."

*The Player had messed up that rule himself.*

Jake tapped his keyboard to wake up his computer. "You go ahead and get the car started. I'm gonna check one more thing and I'll meet you in the parking lot."

Jake watched Billy leave the room before bringing up the database for prisoners in LA County. Would Galecki still be inside for the drug charge?

He looked him up and discovered he'd served less than ten years on that conviction, his sentence reduced for cooperation. Had he survived in prison after collaborating against the cartel? A few more searches indicated he had survived prison life and currently resided in Boyle Heights. Jake jotted down the address. It was his lucky day. He'd rather see Tony in person than try to question him over the phone.

After his lunch with Billy, he dropped his partner at the station and took the car to East LA. He found Tony's address not too far off the freeway and above an office for a moving company—LA Movers and Shakers. Clever.

He parked his sedan next to a moving truck, open in the back, and checked in at the small office. Obviously just a place to direct traffic and schedule moves, the office sported a desk stacked with invoices and littered with paper cups and soda cans. Several metal filing cabinets hunched behind the desk, a bulletin board with a Laker Girls calendar hanging from it at an angle graced one wall and a few dollies were shoved into the corner.

Jake had taken a few steps into the office and turned his head at the sound of footsteps on the gravel in the parking lot behind him.

A young man with dark brown hair and several tattoos marching up his arms clenched his fists at his sides and said, "What do you want?"

Jake stepped aside to let the man bump past him into the office. "Customer service not a requirement in the moving business?"

A blush rose to the young man's tawny cheeks. "You're not here to schedule a move. You're a cop."

"What gave me away?" Jake's lips twisted up on one side.

"The suit, the car out there." The man tilted his chin in an aggressive manner, his beard practically bristling. "I seen enough of you over the years. He's not here."

"You know I'm looking for Tony Galecki?"

"Aren't you always? He done his time. He built this business when he got out. He hasn't done nothing since."

"I believe you." Jake held up his hands, realizing that this young man was most likely Galecki's son—the one who'd been in the car with his murdered mother. Jake swallowed. This boy had been younger than Kyra when his mother had been murdered, but he must've experienced some of the same trauma as she had.

"I'm not here to harass your father. I just have a few questions to ask him about that time—when your mother was killed."

The son blinked. "He ain't got nothing to say about that anymore."

"AJ, let me be the judge of that."

Jake spun around to find Tony Galecki hovering in the doorway, his arms crossed over his wiry frame, his head cocked to the side. Although Galecki had a receding hairline, he'd gathered what hair he did have in a ponytail that hung down his back.

Jake thrust out his hand. "Mr. Galecki, I'm Detective McAllister with LAPD Homicide. I'd like to ask you a few questions about your arrest twenty years ago."

Galecki hesitated before grabbing Jake's hand. "This is my son, AJ."

Jake shook Galecki's hand and then extended it to AJ, who'd stuffed his own hands in his pockets.

"Son, show the man respect."

AJ pulled a hand from his pocket and gripped Jake's briefly before hiding it in his pocket again.

"Do you have a minute, Mr. Galecki?"

"Call me Tony." He jerked his thumb over his shoulder. "AJ, prep that moving van. A crew's taking it out tomorrow morning."

"Yes, sir." AJ squeezed between his father and Jake and left them in the small office.

"Who raised him? Seems like a good kid."

Galecki circled the desk and plopped down on the wheeled chair. "My parents. Lucinda's parents couldn't deal. They blamed me for her death. They're not wrong. What do you want after all this time, Detective? It wasn't a cold case. We all know who did it and why."

Jake grabbed a stool, the only other place to sit, and straddled it. "I was looking at your case recently and noticed you'd made a claim that money had been stolen from you."

Galecki narrowed his eyes and ran a thumb down his mustache. "You wired or anything?"

"This isn't official business, Tony. I'm looking into something else. Nobody has to know about our meeting—not even the cops." Jake circled his finger in the air. "Where'd you get the money to start this business?"

Galecki's lips stretched over his teeth in a grim smile. "A little money I had waiting for me on the outside."

"Drug money?" Jake's pulse ticked slow and heavy in anticipation.

"Hey, I'm not proud of it, man. My stupidity caused the death of my woman. I ain't never getting over that." Galecki lifted his shoulders, and Jake noticed the tattoo on his neck that had been refashioned into the word *Baby*.

Jake knew that tattoo had once been AB for the Aryan Brotherhood. Most prisoners had to swear their allegiance to a gang inside if they wanted to survive, but Galecki seemed like he wanted to disavow all that now.

Jake took a deep breath. "But?"

"But they were offering. You know what I mean? Make the theft charges go away for the cops and get a cut of the money. My parents got the cash and they saved it for me, even though I told them to spend it on AJ."

"Who offered you the deal?"

"The old cop. The one who came to tell me first about Lucinda's murder. He didn't know yet that I was working for the cartel and Lucinda's death was a hit. I don't think he's the one who stole my money, though. It was the drug cops who done that."

Jake licked his lips, his throat dry. "Do you remember the name of the old cop who offered you the deal?"

"Oh, yeah. I remember 'cuz he was good to Lucinda's parents and AJ. He was all about AJ, wanted to make sure he didn't go into the system, you know? He kept in touch with Lucinda's parents and mine to check up on the baby. Good guy—except for the corruption. Never could figure out how a cop like that could cover for someone else's theft—but then, you guys stick together, don't you?"

"What was his name, Tony? What was the name of this cop who told you to lie?"

Tony shrugged. "Detective Roger Quinn."

# Chapter Nine

Kyra bustled into the task force war room and grabbed the back of her chair, shooting a glance over her shoulder at Jake's desk. She blew out a breath and collapsed in front of her computer.

She'd decided she had to confront Jake. If he were snooping around *her* house, she wanted an explanation. She'd cooled off some after talking to Rose yesterday. Maybe he'd had an inkling that Quinn had been murdered, didn't want to worry her and headed over to the house to check out a clue.

Anytime Jake had lied to her or kept the truth from her, it had usually been in her best interests. She could actually say the same about her lies—most of the lies she'd told Jake had been in her best interests, too.

She'd gotten over that once Jake had proven to her time and again that he wanted to stick by her regardless of her mistakes and deceptions. Now she had to do the same for him. If he'd lied to her about going back to Quinn's, it had probably been for a good reason—at least in his mind.

She'd been ignoring his texts, giving herself a cooling off period.

She'd texted Jake back this afternoon, and now he was ignoring her messages. She glanced at Billy on the phone. He'd probably know the whereabouts of his partner.

When Billy ended his call, Kyra sauntered to his desk. "Hi, Billy. I just wanted to make sure you passed my info along to Ashley's family."

"I did. Her brother's in bad shape." His lips twisted. "I can relate."

She took the chair next to his, which happened to be Jake's, and leaned into his space. "Has your PI had any luck yet?"

Billy's younger sister had gone missing several years ago, and he'd recently hired a PI, Dina Ferrari, to help him find out what happened. The second copycat, Cyrus Fisher, had started his spree by murdering two African American women, which had triggered Billy, big-time.

"Dina got a line on a guy the family didn't even know was in Sabrina's life at the time. His name never came up. Dina's tracking him down now. I feel hopeful, but, man, talking to Ashley's brother ripped me apart."

"I'm here anytime you want to talk."

"I appreciate that." He pointed at Jake's desk. "You know where he is?"

"I was going to ask you. I haven't heard from him since this morning. I was…busy, so I didn't answer him. By the time I got around to responding, he'd gone radio silent."

"We had lunch, and then he took the car to look into something, didn't tell me what." Billy snapped his fingers. "Actually, you might be a bigger help to me than J-Mac in this. Some of Ashley's AA group agreed to talk to me about the night she went missing. They're a cagey bunch. Maybe they'll be more forthcoming with a therapist there. You game?"

"Where are you meeting them?"

"At the AA meeting site—a church in Glendale. That's where her brother found her car."

"I'll come with you. I saw clients this morning and figured I'd do some work at the station this afternoon, but as none of Ashley's friends or family has contacted me yet, I might as well go with you."

As they left the war room together, Captain Castillo grabbed Billy's arm. "Where's J-Mac?"

"He's the man in demand, but I don't have a clue." Billy jerked his thumb at Kyra. "Kyra and I are going to talk to Ashley's AA group. Find out if they saw anything unusual that night or noticed a difference in her behavior."

"Good, good." Castillo waved his hand in the air. He barreled into the war room anyway, as if he intended to stake out Jake's desk.

Billy shook his head as they made for the staircase. "That man needs to chill...or retire."

"He has seemed rattled lately." Kyra knew Jake had his own suspicions about Captain Castillo, but he'd never been anything but helpful and nice to her—probably on Quinn's orders.

On the drive to the church, Billy asked her about the funeral plans for Quinn.

Kyra glanced at Billy's profile, his smooth, dark skin displaying not one crease of worry or consternation. Either Jake hadn't told his partner about Dr. Ellis's findings, or Jake had told him to keep the information on the down-low.

Kyra fiddled with her phone in her lap, keeping her eyes downcast. "As far as I know, the autopsy isn't done yet. At least, I haven't been notified. Quinn's attorney, Terrence Hicks, is going to do most of the arrangements with the department."

"I'm sure Terry will do it up right with the bagpipes and everything." Billy clasped her hand briefly. "Going to be hard on you."

"Has been and will be." She sniffed. "Everyone has been great, though, and Quinn himself made it easier on me. He'd been planning for this moment for quite a while."

"Most cops do."

They finished the drive on a lighter note with Kyra teasing Billy about his dating life. He was separated from his wife and had been going out with one of Kyra's friends, a TV reporter, but both Billy and her friend had assured her their relationship was casual.

As soon as Billy pulled up outside the church, their sober mood returned. Most likely, Ashley Russell had been snatched from this parking lot. The cops had no evidence indicating how the killer had taken her.

The area around her car showed no signs of a struggle. Her car itself yielded no clues. But someone had lain in wait for a vulnerable woman, recovering, perhaps emotional, and had taken her away and murdered her.

She exited Billy's car and glanced up at the eaves of the church. "No cameras?"

"Not a one." He gestured toward the side of the building. "The meeting room is over here. Has its own entrance."

Kyra pulled on her jacket as she followed Billy around the corner. A door stood open and Billy poked his head inside the room.

He called out, "Marcia?"

Kyra heard a woman's voice answering from the depths of the room. "That's me. Are you Detective Crouch?"

Billy waved to Kyra. "I am, ma'am. I brought

a therapist with me. Kyra Chase works on our task force."

Kyra stepped through the door after Billy, catching a whiff of coffee and piety. She'd smelled a lot of piety during her stint with one of her foster families. Church every Sunday and hell to pay after at home if the foster mom didn't think you were paying attention at the service or hadn't sung loudly enough or hadn't put your money in the plate. Those parents had been believers, all right—believers in spare the rod, spoil the child. So they'd been quite liberal with the rod, and Kyra had run away from that home so many times, the foster parents had come to believe even God Himself couldn't save her.

Marcia left off fussing over a table filled with cookies and that coffeepot to greet them. "What a wonderful idea to have a therapist working with the police. I think some of us will feel more comfortable with Kyra here."

"Thank you." Kyra shook hands with Marcia, whose round cheeks bunched into a smile.

"Have a seat." Marcia's blue eyes twinkled as she indicated the chairs already in a circle. "I promise, you don't have to confess anything."

"Good, because we're hoping to get some answers from you about Ashley's last meeting here." Billy folded himself into one of the metal chairs.

Marcia remained standing. "Would you like some coffee?"

Both Kyra and Billy declined, so Marcia took a seat next to Kyra. "I feel guilty about Ashley's murder."

Kyra nodded. "That's not uncommon. What do you think you did or didn't do that put her in harm's way?"

Marcia ran her fingers through her curly dark hair, laced with gray. "She was my co-hospitality person. When I couldn't bring the refreshments, Ashley stepped up. I was running late and asked her to fill in. She picked up some coffee and snacks and then stayed after the meeting ended to clean up—that comes with the duties. That's why she was in the parking lot on her own that night. That's why nobody witnessed her abduction."

As they talked to Marcia, a few other people filtered into the room, nervously sidling up to the refreshment table and grabbing coffee and cookies before joining the circle. They didn't introduce themselves, and she and Billy didn't ask. If one of them had something pertinent, Billy could always get the information later.

Billy ran his finger around the circle. "All women? No guys come to this meeting?"

Marcia answered for all of them. "This is a women's-only AA meeting. Some of us find it easier to share with other women. There are men-only meetings, as well. There are meetings for LGBTQ, some for parents, some for singles. Something for everyone to feel comfortable."

Billy hunched forward, elbows on his knees. "The fact that this is a women's-only meeting is published someplace? Someplace public?"

Marcia answered, her eyes bright with fear, as the other women rustled around her. "Of course. There's a website for AA meetings in Southern California. Anyone can see that."

One of the other women on the far side of the circle, her hands wrapped around a Styrofoam cup of coffee, asked, "You think he targeted our group because of that? Do you think any one of us could've been his victim that night?"

"We just don't know." Billy clasped his hands between his knees. "This guy could've been stalking Ashley, knew she came to this meeting and ambushed her. But I'll tell you what. Let me know what time this meeting gets out, and I'll make sure a Glendale PD officer swings around on patrol at that time."

The rest of their conversation with the women gave them nothing. Ashley hadn't been any different that night. None of the women had seen anyone lurking near the church, and every one of them had left before Ashley—and now blamed themselves for it.

How had the killer known Ashley would be the last to leave? Were the women's fears warranted? Copycat Four would've been satisfied with any one of them?

Billy was right. The task force had nothing on this guy yet—even though he'd committed a second murder within twenty-four hours of the first. The Copycat Player Task Force still hadn't released that information. They wanted to protect Piper, make the killer believe he'd gotten his witness.

By the time they left the meeting, the sun had dipped low in the sky and the temp in the shade made Kyra shiver.

She slid into the passenger seat of Billy's car and took out her phone, which she had silenced. She puffed out a small breath when she saw a text from Jake, and then sucked it back in when she read the message.

He asked her to his place for dinner tonight and indicated he had something important to tell her. Had he gotten confirmation from Dr. Ellis? Had he found something the night before in Quinn's house?

Billy punched the ignition. "Everything okay?"

"Heard from Jake finally."

"Did he say where he'd been?"

"No. Do you want me to ask?"

"He'll tell me if it's important."

Apparently, what he had to tell *her* was important. She texted him back that she was on her way to the station with Billy and would drop by his house for dinner.

They hit some traffic on the freeways. By the time they got to the Northeast Division, the shift change had already occurred, and most of the detectives had left the station.

Billy pulled right up to the front door. "Okay if I drop you here? I don't need to go in. I took all my stuff with me, and I'll bring the car home tonight."

"This is fine. Thanks for taking me along, even though we didn't get much out of the meeting."

"I wouldn't say that. He may be hitting up late-night meetings where women are likely to be going out to their cars alone in places that probably don't have security cameras. Every bit helps."

Kyra thanked him again before climbing out of the sedan. Entering the building, she waved at the night sergeant at the front desk. She jogged up the stairs. A smattering of people hunched over their computers or phones in the task force room, and she called out a hello here and there.

She'd left her laptop on her desk when she'd gone to the AA meeting with Billy, and she woke it up now and checked her emails. Ashley Russell's brother, Wade, had contacted her, and she replied to let him know her availability for tomorrow.

As she skimmed through the rest of the messages, Captain Castillo appeared at the door of the war room. He didn't usually stay this late, and his disheveled appearance and dark circles under his eyes signaled he should've gone home hours ago.

Kyra smiled. "You're here late, Captain."

"I was waiting for you, Kyra. Do you have a minute?"

"Me?" She glanced behind her to make sure there were no other Kyras in the room.

"When you're free."

"Just let me wrap up, and I'll drop by your office." He left, and as she logged off her laptop, she mulled over why he'd want to see her. He must want to discuss Quinn's funeral. Soon enough, everyone would know Quinn had been murdered. That would probably double the attendance at his funeral.

She didn't need to return to this room, so she hitched her laptop case over one shoulder and her purse over the other. She trooped down to Castillo's office with both bags banging against her hips.

He'd left the door open in invitation as there were few people left on the floor, but when she stepped inside, he asked her to shut the door. A flutter of trepidation invaded her bones.

She nudged the door closed with her foot and dropped her bags to the floor. When she sat in the chair across from his desk, she gripped the arms.

Captain Castillo spent several seconds straightening items on his orderly desk and then asked, "How are the funeral arrangements for Quinn going?"

Kyra's shoulders slumped, and she uncurled her fingers. He *did* want to talk about Quinn's funeral, not that that discussion didn't pose its own pitfalls. "I'm really not the person to ask. Terrence Hicks is organizing everything right now. I think once he gets certain concessions from the department, he'll present me with choices, and then I'll be more involved in the planning."

He cocked his head. "I haven't heard from Terrence at all yet...or the ME's office. They're not done with the autopsy?"

"The ME hasn't notified me that she's done with the autopsy." She folded her hands in her lap to keep her fingers from fidgeting.

"She?" Castillo's gaze sharpened, and Kyra felt it probing her face.

"Jake mentioned a Dr. Ellis was doing the autopsy, and he called her *she*."

"I know Dr. Ellis. She's thorough and professional."

Would Castillo find Dr. Ellis all that professional if he knew she'd given Jake info on the sly and dropped the word *murder* in his ear?

She cleared her throat. "That's what Jake said. Maybe that's why it's taking a long time."

"You would think with Quinn's history, the autopsy would be a mere formality."

*Except for the shoe, the sock and the needle mark between his toes.*

"I'm happy to say I'm not familiar with the process of an autopsy." She lifted her shoulders. "When I get the word that the examination is complete, I'll contact Terrence, and he'll move forward with the plans."

Castillo fiddled with a pen on his desk, and Kyra waited, the silence stretching between them so tightly she felt as if she could reach up and pluck it. Was that all he wanted to ask her? Why'd he ask her to his office and close the door?

The knock from outside startled them both. Castillo dropped the pen, which rolled to the floor unheeded, and Kyra jumped in her seat, kicking over her bag. The noise snapped the tension in the room.

Castillo called out, "Come in."

When Jake opened the door, Kyra widened her eyes. She hadn't expected to see him until later for dinner.

But if she was surprised, her emotions were nothing compared to Captain Castillo's. His sharp intake of breath caused Kyra to glance at him behind his desk. His mouth had gone slack, and a sheen of moisture had popped out on his forehead. Castillo ducked down to retrieve the pen, his voice sounding muffled. "What can I do for you, McAllister? Surprised to see you here so late."

"Are you?" Jake stepped into the room, clicking the door behind him. "Were you going to tell Kyra the truth, or should I?"

A choking sound came from the captain, and his eyes bulged from their sockets. "He told you."

Kyra jerked her head back toward Jake, his jaw hard, steely resolve vibrating from his body. What was going on?

"If you mean Tony Galecki, then the answer is yes."

"Who the hell is Tony Galecki?" Kyra leaned back from Jake's looming frame, which was suffocating the space in the office.

Castillo closed his eyes for a second, took a deep breath and clasped his hands beneath his chin as if in prayer. "I actually *was* going to tell her."

"Because you knew I talked to Galecki today. Do you have an alert on his file?"

Kyra still had no idea who Galecki was or what they were talking about, but Jake's question pinged Castillo between the eyes. His brown skin flushed deeply.

"I'm sure Galecki told you everything. Why wouldn't he?" Castillo jabbed a finger at Jake. "Are you willing to destroy Kyra's faith in Quinn, the only father she knew?"

Kyra's heart slammed against her rib cage, rattling it, and her clammy hands gripped the edge of Castillo's desk. "What is he talking about, Jake?"

Crossing his arms, Jake leaned against Castillo's office door. "Quinn left me more than those weapons in his will, Kyra."

"Okay." She smoothed her hands over the thighs of her slacks. "Is that why you went back to his place the other night when you told me you were going home?"

His eyebrows jumped. "How'd you…?"

"Rose saw you. What else did Quinn leave you?"

"A crime report—from the night your mother was murdered."

She glanced at Castillo, who listened with closed eyes, his nostrils flared with his heavy breathing. "We have that crime report. *I* have that report."

"You have the revised report, the official report, the report that was filed by Officer Castillo." Jake spread his hands in front of him. "Quinn left me the original report."

Her adrenaline surged, and prickles of anger danced across the back of her neck. "Are you trying to tell me Quinn lied on a police report? That he deliberately changed a report and let it stand as the truth?"

Castillo snorted, and Jake glared at him as he answered, "He did."

Kyra rocketed to her feet, using the arms of the chair as leverage. "Quinn would never do that. He was a good cop, an honest cop."

Jake reached for her, but she reared back. "He would if it meant he could protect you. He was a good cop, but he was a better man."

"Protect me?" She thrust her finger against her chest. "How would submitting a fraudulent police report protect me?"

Jake lifted one shoulder, his green eyes dark and murky. "Because you witnessed your mother's murder that night. Marilyn Monroe Lake saw The Player."

# Chapter Ten

The room spun, and Kyra threw out an arm to brace her hand against the wall. Her lips moved automatically before her brain formed the words. "No, I didn't."

Jake took her free hand in his. "You did, Kyra. It was right there in the report. The attack on your mother woke you up. You stood at your bedroom door and saw the end of your mother's struggle."

"I didn't." She shook her head, and her ponytail whipped back and forth. "Why would Quinn lie about that? I could've described the killer. I could've helped catch him. I was a witness."

Guiding her back to the chair, Quinn said, "Because he saw you, too."

She ended up in the chair with a plop that jarred her teeth. "H-he saw me? That's what I told Quinn?"

"That's what you told *me*." Castillo had slumped in his own chair, his head in his hand. "Then you repeated the story when Detective

Quinn came onto the scene. Quinn told me right then and there that the killer could never know you admitted to seeing him. We changed the report to indicate that you'd slept through the whole thing. You were never listed as a witness, and The Player must've believed you'd forgotten, too traumatized to remember locking eyes with him."

"I *don't* remember. I don't remember any of it." Kyra placed a hand at her throat. "I can't believe Quinn lied, actually changed a crime scene report. And you—" she narrowed her eyes at Castillo behind his desk "—why would you agree to something like that?"

Castillo, his face stamped with anxiety in every line, shot Jake a look. "Ask him."

"That's not important now, Kyra. Just know that Quinn did it to protect you. He didn't want to expose you to The Player's scrutiny. He wanted to keep you off his radar."

"It explains why I *have* been on his radar all these years. He knew I saw him, thought I could ID him, and he wanted to keep tabs on me. He's been testing me during the copycat slayings, making sure I wasn't a viable witness." She chewed on her bottom lip. "Why did he leave that report for you, Jake?"

"He was passing along the torch for your protection to me." He gripped the back of his neck with his hand. "I failed. My first instinct was to honor his wish, but I knew you'd want to know."

"Maybe it was no longer his wish, Jake. Maybe that's why he left it to you instead of Captain Castillo." She tipped her head toward Castillo. "Maybe he knew you'd do the right thing."

Castillo's tongue darted out of his mouth. "Wh-what are you going to do with the information, specifically the information from Tony Galecki?"

"Relax. I'm not going to do anything with it… right now." Jake extended his hand to Kyra. "Let's go to my place. We'll have dinner and talk over everything."

She took his hand, and his warmth and strength gave her courage. She stood up on legs she thought were going to fail her minutes before. Whoever Tony Galecki was and whatever happened between him, Quinn and Castillo, she'd deal with it later. She had some important decisions to make tonight…and Jake would be by her side to help.

They left Castillo to his tormented thoughts and regrets, and Jake walked her to her car.

"Follow me to my house. I have some steaks and red wine and a warm bed."

"And advice? Are you going to have that, too?"

"I don't know about advice, but we can talk it all out." He opened her car door. "I can be your therapist tonight."

She kissed him lightly, and then slid behind the wheel of her car. As she waited for Jake's sedan to pull out of the parking lot, her mind raced in circles. She'd witnessed her mother's murder. She'd seen The Player.

Quinn had been looking out for her the minute he met her. He'd changed a report to protect her. She never would've believed that of him.

When Jake's car appeared, she stepped on the gas and followed him out to the street. When had she forgotten she'd witnessed the murder? She'd been eight years old. She remembered most of that night. She remembered Quinn coming into the room, his suit slightly rumpled, his already graying hair sticking up like he'd just rolled out of bed, his comforting arms around her as she trembled in shock and fear. She even remembered the smell of his aftershave, which he continued to use years later.

A tear trembled on her eyelashes, blurring Jake's taillights ahead of her, and she dashed it away. Quinn shouldn't have risked his career for her. Maybe she would've been able to ID The Player and stop his deadly reign of terror. If Quinn had caught him twenty years ago, he wouldn't be active today, encouraging others to follow in his evil footsteps.

She chose to believe that's why Quinn saved the initial report and left it with Jake. He knew

Jake would do the right thing…and protect her. Once the copycat killings began, maybe Quinn realized she had to know the truth.

But what would she do with the truth?

She followed Jake's car up the winding roads of the Hollywood Hills to his house. When they made it inside, she collapsed on the couch that faced the glass wall overlooking the twinkling lights of the city.

He brought her a glass of wine as she toed off her shoes, and then sat beside her, pulling her feet into his lap. "Did the ride over give you time to process?"

"Not really. I still find it hard to believe Quinn would do something like that. It could've ended his career."

"He had a long career already, and I guess he figured your safety was more important than his job." He drove his thumb into the arch of her foot. "Your safety is important to me, too, Kyra. I told you because you had a right to know."

She lightly tickled the inside of his wrist. "Not because I busted you?"

"I didn't know Rose had ratted me out when I charged into Castillo's office tonight. I just wasn't sure what he was telling you." Jake scuffed his knuckles across his jaw. "I don't trust him."

"Are you going to tell me what he did? Why did he agree to go along with Quinn's decision to scrap the original report and lie?"

Jake pulled his bottom lip between his teeth. "It's not a favorable story for Castillo—but it's not a favorable story for Quinn, either. Are you sure you want to hear it?"

"I've already reached the conclusion that Quinn was not as honest as I thought he was. I might as well hear it all. It's not going to change my opinion of him as the best damned father a girl could've had." She cupped her wineglass with both hands and took a swig, the dark, fruity liquid warming her throat.

"It goes back to an LAPD drug task force called LA Impact. Castillo was on that task force and arrested Tony Galecki, a dealer for the Sinaloa cartel. Quinn had been investigating the murder of Galecki's girlfriend, and the murder investigation dovetailed with the drug task force."

"What does this all have to do with me and my mother's murder?"

"Galecki had been skimming—cutting the drugs, selling more than his allotted amount and pocketing the extra cash. That's why the cartel assassinated his girlfriend."

Kyra hunched her shoulders. "Terrible. Go on."

"When Galecki was arrested, he claimed he had fat stacks, and when the cops couldn't find his money, Galecki accused them of stealing it."

Kyra covered her mouth with her hand. "Castillo stole Galecki's money?"

Jake nodded, his lips pressed together. He obviously didn't want to spill the rest—the part that made Quinn look bad.

She took another sip of wine and cupped it on her tongue before swallowing it and continuing Jake's story for him. "Quinn knew about the theft and made it go away for Castillo as long as he lied about the report."

Jake replied, "Quinn made a deal with Galecki, let him keep a cut of the money, let Castillo keep his, and the future captain kept his mouth shut about the night of your mother's murder in exchange."

"Did Quinn take any of the money?" She folded her hands across her stomach to suppress the butterflies.

"No. He wanted nothing out of the deal except for Castillo to keep quiet about your witnessing the murder."

Kyra slumped against the pillow. Quinn hadn't been the straight arrow she'd always believed him to be, but that didn't matter.

"The worst is over." Jake held up his hands. "That's all I got."

"But that's not all you have." Kyra narrowed her eyes. "You have the original report. Quinn left that, didn't he?"

"Yeah." Jake's Adam's apple bobbed as he swallowed, and he hadn't even taken a sip of wine.

"I'd like to see it, Jake. I need to see it."

"I will hand it over to you on one condition." He waved a finger in the air. "You eat a decent meal tonight. I'm going to grill some steaks, cook potato wedges and toss a salad—and you're going to eat it."

"It's a deal. Gimme." She snapped her fingers, and he lifted her legs from his lap and pushed off the couch.

As he jogged upstairs, probably to retrieve the report from his safe, Kyra took her wineglass to the kitchen and dumped in a little more of the ruby-red liquid, which sloshed up the sides. She had a feeling she'd need something to get through the report—not that she hadn't read its replacement a countless number of times.

Jake returned, a sheaf of papers pinched between his fingers. He placed the report on the coffee table. "I'm leaving it here, and I'm going to make dinner."

"Thanks." She raised her glass in salute and sauntered back to the couch, eying the stack of papers as if it were an explosive device. It just might be.

Jake buzzed around the kitchen, running water, chopping and clanking pans, but the noises couldn't distract her from the words in front of her.

The story unfolded pretty much as she'd read from the dog-eared report she kept in her own safe at home. A female child had called 911, and Officer Carlos Castillo had responded to the duplex in Hollywood. Upon entering the residence, he'd discovered a young girl, sobbing on the phone with the 911 operator still on the line, her hands, legs and feet slick with blood, next to the dead body of a woman she claimed was her mother.

Upon examination of the body, Castillo realized the serial killer The Player had struck again based on the card in the woman's mouth, her missing finger and her death by strangulation. The blood on the child had come from her mother's hand and another cut her mother had suffered from a broken vase, indicating the woman had put up a fight.

Castillo tried to question the child, but she wouldn't or couldn't answer him. He put in a call immediately to Detective Roger Quinn, the lead detective on The Player case. Quinn was in the area and showed up before any other emergency personnel. He was also able to get the girl to talk to him.

Here's where the stories diverged, and Kyra took a gulp of wine before continuing. According to Quinn, the girl reported she was in her bedroom and heard noises. She got up, peeked through a crack in her door—and saw the man who murdered her mother.

She must've made a noise because the man looked up from his gruesome deeds, and his eyes met the girl's. Quinn got a garbled description of the killer from the victim's daughter. The first responders arrived, and the report continued with the familiar sequence of events.

Kyra blew out a wine-scented breath and placed the papers on the polished wood of the coffee table. She sniffed the air and realized Jake was still in the kitchen cooking.

She got to her feet and leaned on the kitchen island to watch him sweep the rest of the chopped veggies into two bowls. "Jake?"

"Yeah?"

"In the report, Quinn mentioned that I gave a garbled description of the killer."

"I know." He stuck the cutting board in the sink and rinsed it off. "Maybe he realized your eyewitness account wouldn't be that useful, and that helped him decide it wasn't worth risking your safety over it."

"Don't make excuses for him. Any eyewitness report would be helpful." She ran a finger around the rim of her glass. "Neither he nor Castillo included any details of my description in the report. What did I claim? A man with red eyes and horns killed my mother? Was Quinn already thinking of chucking my eyewitness account to protect me?"

"You can imagine what he was thinking." Jake

circled the island and put the salad bowls on the table. "Scared, shocked little girl locking eyes with a killer. He didn't want to expose you—especially if your account wasn't going to be helpful. Sit."

She picked up her glass and sat down. She waited until Jake had slid the steaks and potatoes onto plates and set them on the table. When he sat to her left, she grabbed her fork and toyed with her salad. She'd promised him she'd eat, but her appetite hadn't returned since they found Quinn on the floor of his house. The punches had kept coming in quick succession.

The savory smell of the steaks made her mouth water, and she dug into her salad first. The wine, the food—and the company—slowly unwound the knots in her belly, and she was able to cut into her steak with gusto.

She waved her fork dripping with steak sauce. "This is so good. I didn't realize how hungry I was."

"Good, keep eating. You need your strength. The other shoe hasn't even dropped about the cause of Quinn's death."

She dropped her knife, and it clattered against her plate. "Jake, you don't think Captain Castillo had anything to do with Quinn's death, do you?"

He stared into his wineglass as if looking for the answer there. "I admit I suspected it at first, but I don't think he's a killer. He and Quinn must've discussed the report numerous times. I believe Quinn told Castillo that he'd kept the report, and I believe Castillo wanted him to destroy it—for both their sakes. There was no reason for Castillo to believe Quinn was going to come clean about the report."

"Really?" She swirled the mingling fat from the steak and the sauce on her plate with the tines of her fork. "Not even when the copycat killers started operating? We both noticed Castillo's unease when one copycat succeeded the other."

"Castillo may have wanted Quinn to destroy the report, but he knew Quinn wouldn't go public. He wanted to protect you." Jake dug his elbows into the table and balanced his chin on his fists. "I do believe that Castillo is the one who searched Quinn's house, though."

"You're probably right about that." She pushed her plate away. "That was yummy. You're a good cook."

"I have my repertoire. Too bad my daughter's a vegetarian these days, as my repertoire pretty much is this meal."

Patting her stomach, Kyra said, "It hit the spot. I haven't felt this relaxed since…"

She covered her eyes with her hand, and Jake jumped out of his chair and circled behind hers. He placed his hands on her shoulders and said,

"It's all right. We'll get justice for Quinn—one way or another. Finish relaxing on the couch. I'll clean up."

"No, you don't. Look at you." She pinched his dress shirt between her fingers, his sleeves rolled up to expose the end of the tiger tattoo on his forearm. "You haven't even changed out of your work clothes. You get comfortable and I'll do the dishes."

He relented and dropped a kiss on the top of her head. "You twisted my arm."

As he went upstairs, she stacked their plates and rinsed them at the sink. She loaded the dishwasher and cocked her head as she heard the shower upstairs. Imagining Jake's body beneath the stream of water, she almost dropped the dishes to scamper upstairs to join him.

They hadn't made love for a while, and she missed the closeness. She'd been on edge and resentful of Jake for keeping his midnight visit to Quinn's house a secret from her, but his revelations tonight had shored up her faith in him and deepened her love. She needed him more than ever.

She finished cleaning up, poured more wine for Jake, and took her glass to the window, where she swirled the dark liquid and stared at the shimmering lights below. Quinn had risked so much to protect her. She wished she could've protected him in the end. If someone had murdered him, who? Not Castillo. She agreed with Jake. The captain was no killer—corrupt, but no killer.

The Player? She shivered despite the warmth of the wine and food in her belly. Had Quinn known The Player all this time? He never would've turned his back on a stranger in his house—never would've let a stranger into his house in the first place. Had The Player been hiding in plain sight?

She heard a step on the stairs and shifted her gaze from the city lights to Jake's reflection in the glass. He'd changed into a pair of basketball shorts and a white T-shirt. Now she felt over-dressed. She should remedy that.

He made a detour to the counter and picked up the glass she'd left for him. Meeting her eyes in the window, he prowled behind her until he stood at her back, one arm wrapped around her waist.

She inhaled his soapy scent, which could never mask the pure masculine essence that emanated from his body. "You smell good."

He dipped his head and kissed the side of her throat. "You taste good."

She undulated her hips against his pelvis, and he gasped and said, "That's quite a greeting."

Holding her wineglass away from her, she started to turn toward him, but he stopped her and took the glass from her hand. "Let me have that. You, stay right here."

She relinquished her wine, and he took a step back and placed both glasses on a side table. Then he snuggled up against her back again, his hands splaying across her stomach, his tongue tickling the lobe of her ear.

She reached down and steadied her hands against his bare thighs, her back arching. "Not fair. I'm still in my work clothes."

"Do you want me to fix that for you?"

She purred, "If you promise always to be my handyman."

He chuckled in her ear as he undid the first three buttons on her blouse. He loosened the hem of her top from the waistband of her slacks and pulled it over her head, sighing as he plucked at the lacy camisole beneath. "You have to make things complicated for me."

He peeled the camisole from her body and then took care of business with her bra. "Halfway there."

She'd already kicked off her shoes. As Jake fumbled with her slacks, she shooed away his hands and released the button and zipper to help the poor guy out.

He needed no further invitation. He hooked his fingers in her waistband and pulled down her slacks, catching her panties on the way. As her pants pooled at her feet, she stepped out of them and kicked them to the side.

"Now *I'm* overdressed." He made quick work of his T-shirt and shorts and sealed his naked body against hers, his warm skin sending sparks through her veins.

She closed her eyes to slits so she could see Jake's large hands roaming across her naked flesh. He gently eased her shoulders and chest forward, and she braced her forearms against the glass. Then he slipped his hand between her legs.

The coolness of the window contrasting with the hot thumping between her thighs made her gasp. His fingers teased her swollen folds, and she brushed her bottom against his erection prodding her from behind.

He nestled his head in the crook of her neck and nibbled on her collarbone as he continued to stir her to climax. Gritting her teeth, she held her breath, the multicolored lights from the city streets fusing into a rainbow glow. She let out a harsh breath that fogged the window, and then scooped it in again as the tension in her body built to a breaking point.

Shoving two fingers inside her, he stroked her heated flesh on the outside until she exploded. She cried out with her orgasm, bucking against him as she braced her hands against the slick glass.

She still clenched around his fingers, her climax shuddering through her body. He withdrew them and entered her from behind. He thrust into her, and she clawed at the window. He had one arm securely curled around her waist, and she rode him hard, smacking her backside against his pelvis as they rocked together.

His big frame heaved as his climax took him, and he nearly lifted her off her feet. As he slowed his pace and trembled behind her, he hugged her body to his, spooning her from behind, and they slid to the floor together.

Breathing heavily, she reached up behind her and wound one arm around his neck. She turned her head and kissed his salty arm wrapped around her waist. "That was…unexpected."

They'd been mutely enjoying each other's bodies, and her voice cracked with the words.

He pulled out of her and drew her into his lap, his brow furrowed. "Not what you wanted?"

"*Exactly* what I wanted and needed. I just thought we'd head up to your bedroom and slip between the sheets."

"There's still time for that. When I saw you at the window, I had to have you—then, there, now, always."

She snuggled against his chest, her hands resting lightly on his legs straddling her. "Are you sure nobody can see us out there?"

"The only building that reaches this height is that one." He tapped his finger against the glass at a multistory office building across the way and below the Hollywood Hills. Can you see anyone through those little square windows?"

She squinted. "I can barely see the little squares."

"There's your answer—no audience."

She drew a heart in the condensation still fogging the glass. "I love you, Jake."

He made a noise in the back of his throat and pulled her closer, burying his face in her messed-up hair. "I love you, too, and I'll do anything to keep you safe. Maybe I should've never told you about Quinn's deception."

"I know you want to protect me, just like Quinn did, but you were right to tell me. I'm not saying Quinn was wrong to keep the secret, but he was my father. You're my lover, my partner, my equal."

He let out a long breath. "I'm glad you feel that way. Now it's out in the open, and maybe you're safer for it."

"I wouldn't say that." She stroked the hair on his leg.

His body stiffened behind her. "Why do you say that?"

"You know why, Jake."

"I do?"

"Sure you do. You even mentioned it at lunch when you hadn't told me Quinn's secret yet."

His hold on her tightened. "What do you mean, Kyra?"

"I mean, I'm going to undergo hypnosis to bring me back to the night of my mother's murder. I'm going to remember seeing The Player, and I'm going to identify him—and that will put me in danger. Let him try to stop me."

## Chapter Eleven

Jake slurped his lukewarm coffee and glanced across the task force war room over the rim of his cup. He and Kyra had spent most of the weekend together, and Kyra had already warned him she'd be in late, as she had a client in Santa Monica and errands. He didn't press her, but was one of those errands contacting that shrink, or rather, the hypnotist?

She'd mentioned to him that a world-renowned hypnotherapist lived right in their backyard, and one of her colleagues had worked with him on a professional level before. He's the one she'd tagged to help her delve into those memories.

Just like Quinn, Jake had known that the fact Kyra had been an eyewitness to her mother's murder could put her at risk, but nobody today had to know she'd discovered that information. Castillo would keep quiet because it was in his best interests to do so. Jake would keep mum about it, too.

One of the cops on the task force broke Jake's line of sight to Kyra's desk, and Jake refocused his gaze on the eager face, eyes glowing behind a pair of glasses. "What is it, Luberger?"

Luberger slid a photo of a woman's wallet onto Jake's desk. "We think we found Copycat Four's trophy."

Jake lifted the piece of paper by the corner and studied the open wallet. "The driver's license is missing."

"That's right." Luberger drilled a finger against the photo. "It should be right there, and Ashley's brother confirmed she kept her license in her wallet behind the plastic shield. He can't find it anywhere."

"Please tell me Clive got to this wallet before you guys had your paws all over it."

Hearing his name, Clive planted himself in front of Jake's desk, a grim twist to his lips. "I did, but he must've been wearing his gloves when he took the license because there were no prints on that wallet save Ashley's."

Pounding his fist on the desk, Jake said, "I thought this guy would be sloppier than the rest. He had a bad start to his career."

When Jake's phone rang, he held up his finger. "Hold on, both of you, for a second."

When he saw the number for the LA County Coroner's Office on his display, his heart

slammed against his chest. He answered, "McAllister."

"Jake, it's Deirdre. It's going to come out
sooner or later, so I'm giving you a heads-up.
Quinn's tox report came back and he had higher
than normal levels of amphetamines in his system. None of his meds would've caused that.
Given that, the puncture between his toes and
the anomalies of the shoe and sock on that foot,
we're classifying Quinn's death as a homicide."

Although he'd been expecting this, Jake curled
his hand around the edge of his desk. "A homicide made to look like natural causes."

"That's right. My office has already notified
Chief Sterling of our report, but I wanted to tell
you personally."

"Thanks, Deirdre. When are you sending the
report over?"

"It's already been sent to the chief."

He ended the call and was staring blankly at
his phone when Clive cleared his throat.

"Something up, Detective?"

"Yep." Jake pushed up from his desk and
braced his hands on it as he shouted, "Attention,
everyone. Retired detective Roger Quinn was
murdered."

The room exploded with outrage and activity. It was the response Jake wanted. He wasn't
going to wait for the chief or Castillo. He clapped

his hands. "You know what this means, right? This investigation belongs to us, to this task force. There is no way Quinn's murder is not linked to The Player and the copycat killers. The Player must've known Quinn had been offering assistance to our task force, that eventually with our newer technology today Quinn might be able to offer a piece of evidence that we could track back to The Player. It was Quinn who gave us the piece that allowed us to link the copycats directly to The Player. So, let's do this."

At the end of his pep talk, Kyra had sidled into the room, her face white and her eyes round.

Jake strode toward her and grabbed her hand. "You heard."

"I knew it. I always knew it."

"You can't go back to the Venice house today. We're going in and processing it as a crime scene, although I don't want to think about the evidence that might have already been compromised there."

"How did The Player get into Quinn's house? If Quinn didn't know him, maybe The Player sent someone else to do the deed—someone posing as a delivery person."

"We'll figure it out. Everyone is pumped for this one."

Billy sailed into the room, fist in the air. "Hope you all don't plan to get any sleep in the next several weeks. I just heard from dispatch. We have another copycat slaying."

THE LIGHT SMATTERING of rain hit the windshield, and Billy tapped the wipers to whisk it off the glass. "I hope this rain isn't washing away any evidence."

Jake used his fist to wipe the condensation from the inside of the window. "What evidence? They never seem to leave any."

"Not true, my man. He left a witness. He left Piper."

"And all she was able to give us was a hunched-over man in dark clothes and a hoodie."

"Her presence lured him out to take a chance. We'll get him. I'm confident. We nailed the other three, didn't we? The Player trained them, too, and they all made mistakes. Number Four is careless." Billy shot him a glance from the corner of his eye. "The Player's been careless, too. Did he think he could kill Quinn and get away with it?"

"He thought Quinn's death would come back as natural causes, but he messed up by replacing Quinn's sock and shoe incorrectly. That tipped off the ME."

"And you know this how?" Billy raised his eyebrows as he took the turnoff for the Angeles National Forest.

"A little inside information." Jake shook his

head. "Damn, I wish we'd processed that house as a crime scene when we first found Quinn's body. Kyra knew."

"How's she doing? She looked rattled in the war room before we left, but I suppose that's natural. She's had it rough."

"She's coping." Jake sealed his lips after the pronouncement. Billy had no idea how rough it was about to get for Kyra, but nobody, not even his trusted partner, had to know what Kyra planned to do.

It had been a long drive to the dump site, and when Billy pulled up, emergency vehicles clogged the road. The responding officers from the LA County Sheriff's Department had known immediately what they had on their hands, and had cordoned off the area in anticipation of the arrival of detectives from the Copycat Player Task Force.

Now Jake and Billy moved through the scene, snapping gloves on their hands and trudging toward the soggy crime scene tape.

A sheriff's deputy from the Altadena division intercepted them, raindrops beading on his khaki uniform. "Detectives, I'm Deputy Lawson. I was the first on the scene. Early-morning bird watchers discovered the body—same MO as the others—card between the lips, missing finger, manual strangulation, no sexual assault evident."

They questioned Lawson for a few more minutes, and then dove into the crime scene. Jake hovered over the body, his gut knotted. The rain hadn't dislodged or damaged the stiff, glossy playing card in the victim's mouth. The blood beneath her hand where the killer had removed her finger had soaked into the dirt.

Crouching down, Jake reached out to trace the purple necklace of bruising around her throat. Another necklace of shiny gold winked at him, and he hooked his finger beneath the chain and pulled it away from her flesh. This guy took driver's licenses, not jewelry.

A couple of attachments tinkled as he dropped the necklace. He went in for a closer look, cupping the discs in his hand, and he cocked his head. "Hey, Billy, what does this mean?"

Billy squatted beside him and squinted at the medallions. "They have Roman numerals and some writing. What do the words say?"

"Brother, you need reading glasses." Jake nudged his partner with his shoulder and tipped his head to read the words around the circle of the disc. "It says, 'To thine own self be true.' Then around the triangle in the middle are the words 'Unity, service and recovery.'"

Jake's pulse jumped. "Is this what I think it is?"

Billy dipped his head. "It's a recovery chip or whatever from AA."

"Boom. We have our link."

THE FIRST THING Billy did when he got back to the station was contact Marcia from the AA meeting at the church in Glendale. With Jake listening in, Billy gave Marcia a description of their murder victim.

Still on the phone, Billy shook his head at Jake and said, "Thanks, Marcia. If something comes up, be sure to give me a call."

Billy slumped in his chair. "She's pretty sure that description doesn't match any of the members at the women's-only meeting there."

Shrugging, Jake said, "He'd have to be pretty stupid to take his prey from the exact same meeting and location, but he does have some connection to these meetings. Maybe he's met women there before, was able to play on their vulnerability and figured it was a good place to hunt for victims."

"I told you, the guy's sloppy." Billy coughed. "Hey, man, I'm bringing a team of CSI folks to Quinn's house today. The captain asked me to take a lead on this."

"I know. Don't worry about it." Jake clapped Billy on the back. "Castillo sent me a text with the news. Thought I was too close to the situation."

Billy's eyes widened. "He sent you a text? That's cold, man."

Jake brushed it off. The text hadn't surprised

him at all—neither the content nor the delivery. He didn't disagree with Castillo's determination that his relationship with Quinn and Kyra might cloud his judgment and hinder the investigative process into Quinn's homicide, and notification by text suited Castillo's purposes right now. The captain hadn't been alone with Jake since Jake discovered his theft of Tony Galecki's drug money.

It suited Jake's purposes, too. He preferred to keep Castillo off balance.

Billy smacked a piece of paper on Jake's desk. "I made a list for you. These are the most recent missing persons reports. They're all entered, and you can look them up online now."

"I'll do this right away, partner."

Grabbing his jacket, Billy turned toward Jake. "You know I'll keep you posted on everything."

"I know that. Go get our man some justice." Jake held out his fist for a bump and Billy obliged.

When his partner left, taking most of the task force's CSI team with him, Jake pulled out his phone to text Kyra. He'd expected her to be here when he got back, and her empty desk had given him a start.

He breathed a little easier when she responded that she had an appointment with Wade Russell, Ashley's brother. The poor guy had been traumatized by his sister's murder. Hell, Billy was still devastated by his own sister's disappearance after all these years.

Jake had gotten through three reports for women who looked nothing like Copycat Four's victim when a call came through on his work cell from the desk sergeant downstairs. "McAllister. Whatcha got, Lomeli?"

"I have a call on the line from a hysterical woman about her roommate who didn't come home last night. Today, she found her car parked in the place where the roommate was last headed, some church."

A muscle in Jake's jaw ticked. "She was going to church yesterday on a weekday?"

"AA meeting."

"Put her through. What's her name?"

"Remy Tran."

The first thing Jake heard from Remy was a shaky breath and a sob. "H-hello?"

"Ms. Tran? Remy? This is Detective McAllister. Can you tell me everything you told the sergeant?"

She repeated the story she'd told Lomeli, adding that her roommate was supposed to come home after the AA meeting for a get-together at the roommate's house they shared in Alhambra. "I was kind of setting her up on a blind date with one of my friends, and thought maybe she got cold feet. But when she didn't come home the rest of the night, I freaked. Tina never does that. She's not into partying, you know?"

"What does Tina look like, Remy?"

After Remy had given him an accurate description of the woman they'd just found with a card between her lips, Jake swallowed. "What's Tina's last name, Remy?"

"Valdez. Tina Valdez. I'm by her car right now."

Jake shot up in his seat. "Don't touch the car, Remy. You got that?"

"No, no. I haven't touched the car because I know there's something wrong. The stuff from Tina's purse is all over the seat and floor. I can see her phone. She'd never leave her phone, never leave her purse. Then I just heard another body was found at Angeles." She broke down, and Jake couldn't get her to listen to another word for several seconds.

Where was Kyra when he needed her?

When Remy's sobs had tapered off to hiccups, Jake continued in what he hoped was a soothing voice. "Give me the address of the church, Remy, and I'll be out as soon as I can. I'm going to call the Pasadena PD for you because they can get there before I do. Can you hold on for a few more minutes?"

"Y-yes." She recited the church's name and address.

After reassuring Remy again, Jake called the

Pasadena PD and told them to secure the car and the area around it. Then he grabbed his jacket and went in search of a CSI team to send out to Pasadena. Billy had already gathered the A team for Quinn's house, but the LAPD housed a large number of professionals.

He burst into the lab, and a young woman glanced up, her eyebrows disappearing beneath her thick, dark bangs. "Detective McAllister? Clive isn't here. He went out to the Quinn scene."

"I know that. You're…?"

"I'm sorry." She scooted around the table in the center of the room where she'd been hunched over a laptop. "I'm Lori Del Valle. I'm a fingerprint tech, too. I just started last year."

Definitely not the A team.

"I have a possible crime scene in Pasadena. We need to process a car. I need a photographer and a CSI who can vacuum properly and test fluids. Now."

"We have a team." Lori jerked her thumb over her shoulder, her dark eyes shimmering with excitement. "I'll tell them. Address?"

He gave her the address, and she scribbled it down. "The scene is being secured by Pasadena PD. I'll meet you all out there."

Jake strode out of the lab and almost collided with Kyra. She grabbed his arm. "I heard on the news she was another copycat victim."

"Verified. Are you busy right now?"

"Just have some notes to do. Why?"

"I think we located the victim's car. It's at a church in Pasadena."

Her fingers dug into his arm. "Church? Another AA meeting?"

"That's right. The roommate's there, and she's distraught, to say the least. Might help to have you there."

"I'll be right on your tail."

Five minutes later, Jake pulled out of the parking lot and flicked on his strobe lights to cut through traffic faster. The sooner he reached that car, the better.

With traffic slowing in the rain, the trip northeast to Pasadena took him twenty minutes. Kyra wouldn't be there for another fifteen.

Remy Tran had used the term *parking lot* loosely. A small patch of asphalt with spaces for five cars, tops, bordered one edge of a community room at the back of the church. The little red Honda protected by crime scene tape huddled on a gravel strip not meant for parking but used anyway.

Jake looked up at the building when he exited his car. He didn't expect to see cameras, and his surveillance confirmed his hunch. His gaze shifted to a petite woman, her black hair covering her face as her head dropped between her knees. Yeah, Remy needed Kyra, stat.

Jake introduced himself to the PPD cop and flashed his badge. "I have a CSI team on the way. I appreciate your securing this for us."

The cop gave him a thumbs-up. "The fact that this creep is doing his hunting in our area has us ready to go. Anything you guys need from us."

"Have you talked to the roommate?"

"Can't get much out of her. She's destroyed."

As Jake walked toward Remy, her head popped up, and she jumped to her feet, wringing her hands. "Are you the cop I spoke to on the phone?"

"That's right, Remy. I'm Detective Jake McAllister." He gestured to the curb. "Do you want to sit back down?"

"No." She paced away from him a few feet and wiped a hand across her wet and swollen face. "What next? Are you going to take her car away?"

"We're going to get inside first and search it here."

"The car's unlocked now, but it was locked." Remy's hand plunged into her purse, and the keys jangled in her trembling fingers. "I have an extra key. I told you I didn't touch the car, but I pressed the remote to unlock it and it clicked, so I know it was locked. I left it unlocked."

"That's fine. Thanks for telling me."

"C-can I stay here while you look?"

"Of course, but can you do something for me first? You don't have to right away, but if you're up to it, can I show you a picture of the victim we discovered today?"

"Dead?" She covered her mouth with both hands. "A picture of someone dead?"

He'd blundered. "I'll tell you what. There's someone on the way, Kyra Chase, and she's going to sit with you. If you feel like looking at the picture, so we can ID your friend—if it's her—let Kyra know. That's all. No pressure."

She sank to the curb again, wrapping her arms around her knees and bowing her head.

Jake pulled out some gloves and a few bags for evidence on his way to the roped-off car. Head down, he examined the area around the car. Gravel moved easily, and he spotted shoeprints that looked like the soles of Remy's flip-flops. The rain had created a few puddles in areas where divots formed in the gravel. Signs of a struggle.

He stepped over those spots, hoping to retain any evidence, and opened the driver's side door. Tina hadn't left her keys in the ignition, and the killer probably wouldn't have been able to lock up the car with the key fob inside the vehicle. Copycat Four took her keys, which meant he probably had the key to the house she shared with Remy.

He checked the interior of the car and didn't

see any blood or any other disturbances, except the purse. He shook out an evidence bag, plucked up the mostly empty purse with his gloved fingers and dropped it inside. He scanned the contents from the purse that littered the passenger seat and the floor beneath it.

The items represented standard issue for most young women's bags—a tube of lipstick, a small bottle of aspirin, a few pens, random coins—things his own daughter had started carrying in a pocketbook. He squeezed his eyes closed and reached for the wallet.

A few credit cards and a grocery store rewards card occupied the slots, but the plastic enclosure where someone might typically keep a license was empty. He ran his thumb along the plastic, and it slid off. How had he removed the license wearing gloves? Latex gloves like the ones he had on wouldn't have given him enough traction to get that license. He placed the wallet in a separate evidence bag.

He heard a commotion and glanced over his shoulder. The CSI team, including Lori Del Valle, had arrived together in a van, and Kyra had just pulled up in her car. He backed out of Tina's vehicle, clutching the evidence bags.

Back on firm ground, he waved at the CSIs. When they formed a semicircle around him, he pointed at the ground. "We need some photos here. Looks like a scuffle took place outside the car, but I'm not sure the rain and wind left any footprints. The flip-flops belong to the roommate, who discovered the car. You can take her prints, too, to rule them out."

One of the techs he didn't know asked, "Any blood in the car or other bodily fluids?"

"Not that I can see." He held up the evidence bags. "These contain the contents of her purse, and I want particular attention focused on the wallet. He removed her driver's license."

He gave a few more instructions and then cut off Kyra making a beeline to the forlorn roommate hunched over on the curb. "That's Remy Tran. She's really upset. I told her you were on your way. She didn't want to look at a picture of the dead woman."

"I wouldn't think so. She's her roommate, so she probably has pictures of Tina on her phone. I'll have her show you one of those and you can compare it to the deceased."

Jake smacked his forehead. "Of course."

Kyra lowered her voice as they walked toward Remy. "Anything in the car?"

"Not much. Seems like the killer accosted Tina outside the vehicle, and then threw her purse into the front seat before he abducted her. He also snagged her license, or maybe he had her take it out for him."

When they reached Remy, Jake introduced Kyra and left them together. While he waited, he asked the deputy a few more questions, and talked to several of the bystanders who'd gathered in bunches, their eyes narrowed, their whispers hushed.

Kyra waved him over, and he approached her and Remy, who had at least stopped crying and had gotten to her feet.

"Show him the picture of Tina, Remy." Kyra patted Remy on the arm.

Bracketing her phone with trembling fingers, Remy held out her phone to Jake.

Jake studied the two smiling young women, and his gut rolled. The woman next to Remy had shoulder-length brown hair and expressive brown eyes…and she now lay on a slab at the coroner's office.

His gaze shifted from the photo on the phone to Remy's tear-filled eyes. She knew already, had known from the moment she'd heard about the body and found her roommate's car on the side of this church. "I'm sorry, Remy."

Remy sagged, and Kyra caught her before she sank to the ground. Jake knew Kyra could handle this woman's grief a lot better than he could, so he turned back to Tina's car.

The tech's vacuum whined as it sucked up fibers and fragments from the back seat of the car, to be analyzed later. Lori, the fingerprint tech, hopped out of the van and strode toward him.

"Detective McAllister, I dusted the purse and the wallet."

"Really?" He raised an eyebrow at her. "I thought you'd just take those back to the station to wait for Clive."

"You know, Clive—" She shook her head. "Never mind. You said the wallet was important, so I thought we could take care of it here."

This one was ambitious. He'd have to warn Clive to watch his back.

"Okay, that's great. Thanks." He started to pivot, and she stopped him with a hand on his arm.

"The thing is, Detective McAllister, I found something on the plastic shield of the wallet. Someone left a latent print…and it didn't belong to Tina."

## Chapter Twelve

Sitting across from Jake at the Uncommon Grounds coffee house, Kyra listened to him berate himself with a curve to her lips. That's one of the things she loved about him. Most men would've glossed over his interaction with Lori Del Valle without a second thought.

"I just dismissed Lori, didn't expect her to have anything, and she turns up with that print. I'd been thinking of her as second-rate all along when I couldn't get Clive. Even worse, I suspected her of playing office politics when it sounded like she was going to criticize Clive." He ran a hand through his dark hair, which stood up on end. "Do you think I did that because she's a woman?"

"You have a lot of strong females in your life, starting with your daughter. I think you underestimated Lori because you thought of her as part of the B team when Billy took all the CSI first-stringers to Quinn's. Face it. You had low expectations of the entire team, regardless of their gender."

"You're probably right. That just makes me an ass." He swirled the dregs of his coffee and took a sip.

"I mean, when you growled at me for joining the task force, I didn't think it was because I was a woman." She lifted her shoulders and winked. "I knew it was because you hated therapists."

"Definitely an ass." He rubbed his thumb on the back of her hand. "Speaking of therapists, did you reach that Chai Gellman character?"

"His name is *Shai* Gellman and he's a renowned hypnotherapist, not a character." She rapped his knuckles with a plastic spoon. "I left him a message, but he hasn't responded yet."

"You're sure you want to do it?"

"Of course I do." Kyra tapped her head. "Those memories are buried in there somewhere, and I want access to them. Look, Quinn may have been overreacting from the beginning. It doesn't sound like I had much to offer in the way of a description of The Player, and maybe I don't know."

Jake said, "I want to be there with you when you go."

"I'd like that, but you know it's not all going to come to me in one appointment. It could take several sessions, and it might not work at all."

"I'm prepared for that. Are you? Maybe we

won't need it. Maybe the CSI A team will gather enough evidence at Quinn's house to find his killer and ID him as The Player."

"Maybe you should've sent the B team to Quinn's instead of the first team." She planted her elbows on the table. "What did you mean when you said Lori Del Valle criticized Clive? I've never heard of anyone criticizing him before."

"Did I say 'criticize'?" Jake popped the lid off his coffee and stared inside the cup as if trying to read tea leaves instead of coffee grounds. "She didn't exactly do that. It was during one of my finer moments when I told her I'd expected her to bring the wallet back to the lab at the station for Clive, rather than dust for prints herself. She started to say something about Clive and then backed off, so it seemed as if she was going to badmouth him. She could've just been thinking he'd be busy with the other crime scene. Anyway, Clive trained her well, and she lifted the latent print off the wallet."

"And it's not Tina's."

"It's not Tina's. We also have the AA connection. I didn't get a chance to tell you." He grabbed his work phone, which he'd been toying with ever since they sat down for coffee to wait for Billy to get back from Quinn's, and tapped it a few times.

"Tina was wearing her AA anniversary medallions at the time of her murder."

Kyra leaned over the table to look at the picture on Jake's phone. Her pulse jumped as she noticed the purple bruises around Tina's neck beneath the gold chain of the necklace. Yeah, it's a good thing Jake hadn't shown the picture of Tina's dead body to Remy.

He cupped the phone in his hand again. "That's why the location of the car piqued my interest. I knew we were probably looking at another AA meeting abduction."

"You called that in on the way over here?" She and Jake had headed straight to Uncommon Grounds after the crime scene. It had been too late for lunch and too early for dinner, and Jake needed to decompress after searching Tina's car.

"Called that in and asked one of the task force officers to track down the meeting Tina attended, and to see if he can schedule a group get-together like the one you and Billy had with Ashley's group. I also asked Lori to send the print over to Officer Reppucci so she could enter it into AFIS, the national fingerprint database."

"You're closing in on this fourth copycat." She thudded a fist against her chest. "I feel it here."

When Jake's phone rang in his hand, they both jumped. He answered after the first ring. "How'd it go, Billy?"

As Billy rambled on the other end of the line, Jake's face, tense with anticipation, relaxed.

Kyra sat back in her seat and finished her coffee. It didn't sound promising from Jake's side of the conversation, but they'd just gotten started. Evidence had to be hauled back to the lab and examined and tested. When Jake asked Billy about the misplaced glass in the cupboard, she held her breath, but Jake's face told her nothing.

When he ended the call, he slammed the lid on his cup. "Not much, as you could probably tell."

"Clive got the glass I noticed when we were last there?"

"He bagged it. I don't think he dusted any items there except for windows and doors."

"Unlike the enterprising Lori." She grinned, wrinkling her nose. "Stop beating yourself up over that. Just apologize to her, and that'll go a long way."

Jake lifted his empty cup. "Are you ready? Billy and I have a lot to discuss. I have to fill him in on the identification of Tina Valdez and the evidence from her car."

"I'm ready."

When they got back to the station, Jake and Billy put their heads together, and Kyra sat in front of her computer to follow up on a list of Tina's friends Remy had given to her. Her cell phone buzzed, and she recognized Dr. Gellman's number.

Turning her back to the busy room, she scooted her chair toward the corner. "Hello, this is Kyra Chase."

"Kyra, this is Shai Gellman returning your call."

"Thank you for calling me back, Dr. Gellman."

"Shai, please. How can I help you?"

In a low voice, she explained she had some traumatic childhood memories she wanted to re-claim. She'd get into the details with him if he accepted her as a patient.

"Are these memories of events you suspect oc-curred or ones that you know occurred and can't recall?"

"I know they occurred, and I can't remember them—it. It was one memory in particular. I re-call the events surrounding the memory but not that one piece."

"Is there someone alive who can verify the memory for you?"

*Only if you count a serial killer who'd rather see me dead than remember.* "No."

"How old were you, Kyra?"

"I was eight years old."

Shai took a deep breath. "I'm not going to lie to you or pretend I don't know who you are. I fol-lowed your story last month from Sean Hughes's blog, so I know about your past. I know your mother was a victim of The Player twenty years ago, and I know you killed a foster father in self-defense. Is this memory from one of those two incidents?"

Kyra bit her lip. "The first. Does that make a difference?"

"It doesn't make a difference to me. I just didn't want you to come in here under false pretenses and then discover later that I knew all about you. We need to have trust between us. You're in the field, so you understand that."

"Thank you for telling me. It doesn't matter to me, either. Is this something you think you can help me with?" Kyra sucked in her bottom lip and stared at a spot on the wall.

"I do. I'd like to help you. I can see you as early as tomorrow, as I just had a cancellation. Will eleven o'clock work for you?"

Her gaze wandered toward Jake's desk, where he and Billy were still yakking. Jake would never be able to make an afternoon appointment, and she'd promised him he could come along. "Something later in the day would work better, the later the better, actually. I have my work on the LAPD task force and my own clients to see. It doesn't have to be tomorrow."

"Hold on." Shai clicked on a keyboard as Kyra

held her breath. "I'll tell you what. I can see you at five o'clock tomorrow, if that works."

"That's perfect." Having notoriety helped in the strangest ways, but she'd take it.

When she got back to her email, she paused as she noticed a message from an unknown address. Her breath caught in her throat as she clicked on it, and then her breathing returned to normal when she saw the message from a therapist she'd contacted for a family member of one of Mitchell Reed's victims. The therapist had wanted to let Kyra know that she'd scheduled her first appointment with the client.

Kyra didn't know if she should expect any more communication from The Player. During the first three copycat slayings, The Player had been in contact with her, posing as someone else, of course—teasing, tormenting and torturing her about her past. He'd been quiet so far, but she didn't know if it was because they'd finally identified him as The Player or if he had something else planned for her.

As Kyra responded to the therapist's email, Morgan Reppucci, one of the few female officers on the task force, walked by her desk and squeezed her arm. "Lori Del Valle just finished prepping the fingerprint she took from Tina Valdez's wallet for me to run through the Automated

Fingerprint Identification System. Keep your fingers crossed."

"Can I tag along when you pick it up?" Kyra scooted her chair back from her desk and snapped her laptop closed. She didn't know if Jake had gotten the opportunity to apologize to Lori for making assumptions about her. Not that Kyra was Jake's apologist, but she didn't want Lori to have a bad opinion of him. She wanted to see the print, anyway.

"Come on." Morgan crooked her finger at Kyra. "I'm excited that J-Mac gave the task to me. Of course, we haven't had much luck with prints yet. Jake did find that print from Copycat Two, Cyrus Fisher, but we couldn't match it in the system. What's weird about that is Fisher must've submitted false prints for the secret clearance he held at the aerospace company where he worked. That definitely would've come up in AFIS."

Kyra followed Morgan into the lab, where a young woman with glasses and dark hair scooped into a low chignon sat at a table. She flushed when she looked up, which made her look younger. Kyra couldn't blame Jake too much for thinking she might be too green to handle the job.

Scoping out the room, Kyra asked, "Where's Clive?"

Lori pulled her glasses off. "He came back with a ton of prints from Quinn's house, started working on those and then had to leave for a doctor's appointment. I know how to prep a print to run through AFIS."

Ouch. Did Jake's dismissal still sting? Kyra smiled. "Obviously—you're a rock star. Detective McAllister was impressed you took the initiative and dusted that wallet in the field. Who knows? We might still be waiting for Clive to get back from the doctor."

"He told me, *and* he apologized for dismissing me, but I didn't really take it like that. Clive keeps a tight grip on this department, and I'm sure he's communicated that to Detective McAllister. Anyway, glad I could help." Lori hopped off her stool and thrust out her hand. "By the way, I'm Lori Del Valle. You're Kyra Chase, right? And I know Officer Reppucci."

As Kyra shook Lori's hand, Morgan said, "Call me Morgan. Us ladies have to stick together in this field. Is it ready to go?"

"You're emailing the request to AFIS, correct?"

"I am." Morgan wandered to the table and peered over Lori's shoulder. "Nice. It's pretty clear."

"I think it is." Lori tapped the table next to the prepped print. "I'm going to scan this and email it to you, Morgan. You can use that format for AFIS."

Kyra glanced from one woman to the other. "Is it true a match can come back within an hour now?"

Lori nodded. "If there's a rush on it, and there's always a rush for prints from a murder scene, especially a serial killer case like this. I'm sure Detective McAllister already put in the request for this print."

"He did." Morgan pumped her fist. "Let's do this."

Kyra and Morgan returned to the task force room, where Morgan perched in front of her computer to await Lori's email, and Kyra looked through the family contacts for Tina Valdez that Remy had sent her. Remy needed as much help as Tina's family would. Finding Tina's car and discovering that she'd been murdered had wrecked Remy.

About forty-five minutes later, a vibration rippled through the room, and Kyra jerked her head up. She narrowed her eyes as she watched Morgan talking to Jake and Billy, her face alight, her shoulders pulled back.

She'd done it. They had a match.

Within minutes, Jake and Billy grabbed their jackets. Before he left the war room, Jake winked at her.

A few other officers had left with the detectives, but Morgan remained at her desk, so Kyra scurried across the room and huddled next to her. "The fingerprint matched one in AFIS?"

"It did." Morgan twisted her head around. "It's not a secret...except from the press, of course. Jake and Billy just went out to surveil the guy— check out his home and workplace. They don't want to tip him off yet."

"Who is he?"

"His name is Adam Walker. He lives in Glendale, so he's definitely in the area of the abductions, and he works at an IT help desk."

Kyra blew out a breath. You just never know about anyone these days. "Is that where his prints came from? His job?"

"Not that job. Apparently he used to work in construction and did a job at a school. Most licensed, bonded construction companies fingerprint their workers if they have a project at a school and are around kids. Maybe he forgot his prints were on file for that job."

"Or maybe he never intended to leave his prints when he murdered these women." Kyra held up both of her hands with her fingers crossed. "Let's hope he's the guy and the task force can stop him before he commits a fourth murder."

Jake and Billy hadn't returned by the end of the day. They must still have Walker under surveillance. They wouldn't want to play their hand yet in case Walker led them to more evidence.

As she walked down the hallway to take the stairs, Captain Castillo called out to her from his office. She poked her head inside, and he waved her into a chair.

She shut the door behind her. "Are you sure you don't want to talk to Jake?"

"I just want to ask you what you're doing about that information?"

Did she owe it to Castillo to tell him her plans? He'd kept Quinn's secret all this time, although for personal reasons, so she supposed she owed him something. She took a deep breath. "I don't know what Jake's doing, but I'm going to see a hypnotherapist and try to recover that memory. I don't know if it'll work or not, but I need to give it a try."

"I think that's a good idea. I'm not sure it will help the case, but I think it's something you need to do." The captain rubbed his chin. "If the rest of it gets out, it's going to hurt Quinn's legacy."

Kyra held up her hands. "I have nothing to do with that, Captain Castillo."

Thankfully, his phone rang and he dismissed her from his office.

She had no clients, and Quinn's house was still off limits to her, so she headed to her apartment in Santa Monica when she left the station. Jake's daughter, Fiona, texted her while she was driving regarding her interview. When Kyra got home, she called her.

"Hi, Fiona. Do you want to ask me those questions now?"

"Do you have time?"

"As long as you don't mind some answers between chews. I'm going to eat while we talk, if that's okay."

Fiona paused. "Is my dad there?"

"Your dad is working."

"As usual." Fiona snorted. "I'm going to record our conversation so I can get quotes later. Is that okay?"

"That's fine with me."

Kyra spent the next half hour eating leftover pasta and answering questions about her career. As Fiona started to wrap up the interview, Kyra asked, "Do you think being a therapist or psychologist is something you'd like?"

"Sounds interesting." Fiona paused. "Does listening to people's problems all day make you depressed?"

"No, because by talking about their problems, they're taking the first step toward healing, and that's exciting. Does that make sense?"

"I get it. It's like when my friends are upset over a boy or something and they talk about it, they usually end up laughing about it and plotting their revenge."

Kyra choked on her water. "Yeah, something like that."

The conversation put a smile on Kyra's face that didn't go away as she cleaned the kitchen and fed Spot. Twenty minutes after she ended the conversation with the daughter, the father called her.

She answered the phone. "Busy afternoon?"

"Busy and frustrating. We went to the suspect's work location first and contacted his supervisor, who told us he left early that day for a doctor's appointment. So we left and did a stakeout at his house, a place he rents alone, but no luck there. His car wasn't in the driveway, and it didn't look like anyone was home. The car could be in the garage, but no lights came on in the house, and there was no activity."

"Morgan told me his name. Maybe Walker's sick and went to bed when he got home from the doctor's visit."

"Maybe. Billy and I called it a day, and two other detectives in an unmarked vehicle are taking over the stakeout. We also have an APB on his car, but with instructions to call it in, not to pull it over. Again, we don't want to tip him off or spook him."

"At least if he is holed up in his house and decides to go on any late-night hunting expeditions, he'll have a tail."

"Exactly. Any activity in the war room after we left?"

"Nope. Seems like everyone got down to business when you and Billy left, doing whatever you instructed them to do." She cleared her throat. "I did have a conversation with Captain Castillo before I left. I told him about my plan to uncover that memory."

"Castillo isn't going to tell anyone."

"He wanted to know what you planned to do."

"I don't even know yet."

Kyra told Jake about the interview with his daughter and about the appointment with Shai the following day. He assured her he'd come with her if he wasn't sitting on Walker.

The rain started pattering against the window, and Spot yowled at the front door. Kyra swung it open for the mangy cat and said, "You're getting wimpy in your old age, Spot. What's a little rain?"

The cat slipped into the apartment and curled up on the edge of the carpet that led into the living room. Spot wasn't into naked affection.

Kyra turned on the TV and settled on the couch with a cup of tea. When a text came through on her phone, she figured it was one of the McAllisters. She swept the phone from the coffee table and read the text from an unknown number, her heart tripping over itself in her chest.

Do you want to find Walker?

She responded.

Who is this?

The sender answered with an address in Hollywood and a warning.

No lights and sirens.

What did that mean? If she called the police, Walker would be gone? Jake had indicated Walker didn't know they were onto him. He and Billy hadn't rushed in with guns blazing. They'd wanted to surveil him first, trip him up, gather more evidence. One print on Tina's wallet wouldn't convict Walker.

Why had this anonymous tipster contacted her? How did he know her, her number, or that she even knew about Walker? Chewing on her bottom lip, she studied the texts.

Only one person had her number and had been contacting her regularly throughout the killing sprees of each copycat. Had The Player surfaced again to give her a heads-up about Walker? Why? Why would he want to reveal one of his minions to her?

She wouldn't call the police, but if The Player

thought she'd come alone, he hadn't been paying attention. Of course, if she thought Jake would invite her along, *she* hadn't been paying attention. She'd have to time this just right.

She bounced up from the couch, turned off the TV and put her mug of tea in the sink. Then she shimmied out of her flannel pajama bottoms and stepped into a pair of dark jeans. She pulled a T-shirt over her camisole and slipped her feet into some soft-soled sneakers.

Stepping over Spot, who gave her the evil eye, she grabbed a black jacket with a hood from the hall closet and pocketed her weapon. She nudged Spot with the toe of her shoe. "You, out."

The cat stretched and flicked his tail at her, but he followed her and stepped into the drizzle when she opened the door. She locked up and headed for her car—next stop, Hollywood.

She'd plugged the address the text had given her, ignoring the 15 at the end of it, into her phone's GPS and followed the directions. Over thirty minutes later, she cruised into Hollywood and obeyed the voice from her phone that took her to a side street off Hollywood Boulevard. Two dilapidated motels occupied one side of the street, and she identified the second one on the right as her destination.

The number following the directions now made sense; 15 was the number of the motel room. She rolled past the entrance to the small parking lot, overgrown with bougainvillea, the petals from the flowers sticking to the wet pavement. Two palm trees guarded the office, the fronds littering the walkway to the sagging screen door.

She passed the motel and did a U-turn at the end of the block, heading back toward the lights of the boulevard. She snatched her phone from the outside pocket of her purse. Jake couldn't keep her away now because she was already here.

Her phantom texter hadn't contacted her again. Was he watching her? She pulled her gun from her pocket and placed it on the console. Then she called Jake.

"Hey, I was just thinking about you, too."

She hated to crash his good mood. "Jake, I got an anonymous text about Walker. I'm guessing you didn't."

"I did not. Anonymous? Is La Prey back?"

Glancing in her rearview mirror at the darkness of the street behind her, she said, "We both know the guy who's been calling himself La Prey is The Player. Listen, he gave me an address for Walker in Hollywood. It's a run-down motel."

Jake drew in a sharp breath. "How do you know that from an address? Did you look it up online?"

"I'm sitting across the street from it." Her muscles tensed.

He didn't explode, but he did mutter a few choice curses under his breath. "Tell me you did not go into that motel."

"I didn't. I'm waiting for you. The texts also warned me not to call the cops, but you don't count because he had to know I'd contact you. You don't want to careen in here with patrol cars on full alert anyway, right?"

"You could've called me and stayed in Santa Monica."

"Naw, I can't do that, Jake, and you know it. I'm in this up to my eyeballs."

"Give me the address and sit tight. Do you have your gun?"

"Of course."

"Keep it handy, and if you're parked in an isolated area, move."

She gazed over the top of her steering wheel at the lights of the busy boulevard. "I'm facing Hollywood Boulevard."

"I'm on my way."

He ended the call, and she expected him in about fifteen minutes. He knew those winding roads in the Hollywood Hills like the back of his hand.

When she saw the motorcycle zip onto the side street fourteen minutes later, she finally relaxed her clenched muscles. He walked the Harley she'd inherited from her foster brother and sold to him up to her window.

She buzzed it down, and Jake flipped up the visor on his rain-spattered helmet. He jerked his thumb over his shoulder. "It's that dump?"

"That's it. Room number 15."

"I suppose it won't do any good to ask you to wait in the car."

"None at all." She grabbed her weapon from the console and flipped up her hood.

She waited while Jake parked his bike in front of her car. He took her arm and they crossed the street, looking like two ninjas all in black.

Jake bypassed the front office and counted the numbers nailed to the doors. Some had fallen off, but they located number 15 around the corner of the parking lot.

Jake's step faltered. "That white car out front is Walker's. Now, I'm going to insist that you stay back so I can get a handle on things here. It looks like I can get a look into the room from the gap in the blinds."

"Okay, it's all yours." She took several steps away from the door and wandered toward the back of the motel. Two more rooms rounded out this side of the building, and then the back of the motel faced an alley and a patch of wild growth that could've been another parking lot.

The wind lifted the ends of her hair and carried the scent of the wet asphalt through the air. She wrinkled her nose at the smell of garbage. A dumpster hunched where the pavement met the overgrown weeds.

The hair on the back of her neck quivered, and she clutched the gun in front of her. She crept forward on silent feet, holding her breath, the stench getting stronger as she approached the dumpster. Standing on her tiptoes, she flipped back the hard plastic lid, and peered inside at the trash and flattened cardboard boxes with the flashlight on her phone.

She went down on her heels and staggered back a few steps, the light from her phone picking out something behind the dumpster in the long grass.

With her gun leading the way, she circled the dumpster and choked. A man, his head sticky with a dark substance, lay on his back, one arm extended to the side, his eyes wide open.

But Adam Walker couldn't see anything anymore.

## Chapter Thirteen

The scream came from outside, not inside the neat motel room, and Jake reared back from the window. He spun around, his heart thundering in his chest, but Kyra wasn't where he'd left her.

He rounded the corner of the building, where a door to one of the rooms cracked open, throwing a sliver of light onto the buckled pavement. He hadn't imagined the scream. Others had heard it, too.

Heading for the back of the motel, his gun clutched in his hand, he took the final corner and stumbled into an alley. He spotted Kyra next to a dumpster, her hand raised, her face a pale oval beneath the hood of her jacket.

He rushed toward Kyra, and she pointed behind her, wordlessly. He smelled the body before he saw it. It hadn't been there long, but the rain had ripened the flesh for decomposition. Before approaching it, he yelled over his shoulder, "Call 911."

With Kyra's steady voice in the background,

Jake peered at the face, the light from his cell phone illuminating the one side of the man's face not covered in blood. He had an exit wound on the right side of his forehead. He'd most likely been shot in the back of the head, execution style, and he'd spun onto his back maybe in midturn, or the killer had rolled him over.

His fingers itched to dig into the man's pocket for his wallet to confirm his identity, but Jake hadn't brought any gloves with him and he didn't want to muck up this crime scene. He rose to his feet and called Billy. His partner had already heard Kyra's 911 call, so Jake said, "I think we found Adam Walker."

An hour later, Jake waded through officers from LAPD's Hollywood Division and his own task force to reach Kyra standing by the motel's front office, now awash in white light. Once the sirens blared on the scene, several of the motel's guests had ventured from their rooms, some peeking out from behind their doors and others hanging on the fringes of the scene, asking questions.

When he reached Kyra's side, he asked, "Are you doing okay?"

"I'm fine. Nobody told me directly the dead man's identity, but I'm guessing he's Adam Walker." She raised her eyebrows at him hopefully.

"It is Walker. Not only did we find his driver's license in his wallet, we found Ashley Russell's and Tina Valdez's licenses. He's our guy."

Kyra's shoulders slumped a little with the verification, but she continued to twist her fingers in front of her. "Why'd he do it, Jake? Why did The Player rat out one of his own?"

"I've been thinking about that ever since you called me. Remember the other copycat killers, and how they acted? Cannon pretty much chose death by cop. He had to know I was going to shoot once he threatened you with that knife. Fisher actually did kill himself with that cyanide tablet, and do you recall Mitchell Reed's question when we burst in to take him down and rescue you?"

She worried her bottom lip. "He said something like, 'Did he send you?'"

"Yeah, I think he meant The Player. He'd told The Player where he was holding you. He wanted special props for capturing The Player's favorite plaything—you. But in the end, he knew The Player would rather see him dead than arrested." Jake jerked his thumb over his shoulder. "Same thing here. He knew we were closing in on Walker, so he took him out before we could get to him."

"How did he know? The task force never announced Walker as a suspect."

Jake shrugged. "Maybe he was watching Walker's place. Maybe he made me and Billy earlier. Maybe Walker noticed us and told The Player—big mistake." Jake circled his finger in the air. "He just checked in to this dump today. He was on the run, but he couldn't outrun The Player."

Kyra said, "I offered up my phone with the text messages on it, but nobody seemed interested. Are you just assuming he sent those messages from a burner phone? Shouldn't you check? Jordy Cannon stole a phone to make a call about the body he left in Malibu Canyon where the fire was raging, and it led you to a location and eventually his capture—I mean, death."

"We already know where the messages came from, Kyra. The Player sent them to you from Walker's cell phone."

"Oh." She folded her arms over her midsection. "Did any of the other guests see anything? Hear anything?"

"The only thing they heard was your scream when you discovered Walker out back. The gun must've had a silencer." He cocked his head and asked the question that had been bothering him since that scream. "Why'd you go back there? What led you to the body? The stench wasn't strong enough yet to reach the motel."

"I can't tell you. It was as if something was pulling me around the back, to the dumpster and beyond." She placed a hand at her throat. "It's as if The Player and I have this connection."

He curled an arm around her shoulder and pulled her close. "That's going to end. I'm going to make sure of it."

"*I'm* going to make sure of it." She flipped up her hood as the clouds above ushered in another spate of rain. "I forgot to tell you that I have an appointment with Dr. Gellman tomorrow at five. Can you make it? You won't be watching for Walker anymore, but you don't have to go."

"I want to go with you. Five is good. Is he closer to your place or mine?"

"Closer to mine. His office is in Brentwood."

"I'll try to be there for you, but we'll be busy tomorrow trying to tie Walker to the three murders. Thank God this guy was held to three."

"I guess we have The Player to thank for that, but then he was partly responsible for the murders of Ashley, Tina and Erica." She squeezed his arm. "Don't worry if you can't make it to the appointment. You can't come inside during the hypnosis, anyway, and I promise to tell you all about it. Shai warned me that it might take several sessions. It's not like I'm going to remember everything after being under just once."

Jake shook his head. "I would hate that—someone in my brain, having control over me."

"It's not exactly like that." She pulled her jacket

close. "Are you done here? I think I am, right? I've given my statement, offered up my phone. I can't say I feel sorry for the guy."

"Nobody's asking you to." He placed his hands on her shoulders. "Can I ask you to wait a minute? I have a few things to wrap up, and then I want to see you home."

"Jake, don't be ridiculous. It's late, it's raining, you're on a motorcycle. I'll be fine. I have security cameras at my place, strong locks and a gun. If The Player wanted me, he could've ambushed me when I got to the motel without you."

"Yeah, about that." He clenched his jaw. He knew it wouldn't do any good to get on her about her risky behavior. She had a stake in this case, a...connection to The Player. She felt entitled to know every part of the investigation and to be involved in it. She *had* been involved until this point, and there was no way she'd back off now.

She tugged at his sleeve. "You can walk me to my car."

He blew out a breath that fogged in the chilly air. "It's the least I can do."

They wended their way through clutches of people, including the press, and crossed the street without anyone following them. Jake turned and surveyed the people on the sidewalk in front of the motel. Was he here? Had The Player stayed to view his handiwork? They'd been taking the videos at every crime scene since the first copy-cat killer and hadn't been able to identify anyone who'd been at more than one of them—outside of the cops, CSI and media. Why would tonight be any different?

Kyra unlocked her door and turned to face him. "I'll call you when I get home."

He watched her drive toward Hollywood Boulevard and turn left. Why did The Player have to keep pulling her into his sick games? He suspected The Player might be yearning for the notoriety he'd shunned twenty years ago. Maybe The Player thought it was time to get caught—and Jake was ready to oblige the evil bastard.

THE FOLLOWING DAY, Jake stood in the middle of Adam Walker's house in Altadena. Copycat Four had left in a hurry—dishes in the sink, perishable food in the fridge, mail on the floor, and closets and drawers gaping open in the bedroom.

Clive was picking up prints throughout the house, and Geoffrey, another member of the Forensics team, was sifting through Walker's dirty clothes in the hopes of finding some DNA from the victims. They'd towed Walker's car from the motel parking lot, and the techs had already notified Jake that they'd discovered one long strand of brown hair—Tina's?

Brandon Nguyen had already secured Walker's

laptop from the motel room and had started a forensic analysis on it. Jake was confident they'd be closing the case on Copycat Four shortly.

But that sense of satisfaction eluded him. He was happy to offer justice to the families, but the main perpetrator was still roaming the streets, still had Kyra in his sights. The Player might be setting up a fifth copycat right now. He'd clearly abandoned Walker, had, in fact, killed Walker, but it didn't mean he'd given up his diabolical school for serial killers.

When he checked the time on his phone, he grimaced. Kyra had that appointment at five o'clock today, and he'd wanted to be there for her, but it wasn't looking good. He knew she'd been busy today with Tina's family and trying to set up a group session for the family members of all the victims. Once they'd learned a few months ago that Kyra herself was a family survivor of The Player, their trust in her had gone through the roof. They shared that bond.

"Look at these," Billy called from across the room and bobbled some tokens in the palm of his hand.

"What are those?" Jake strode across the room and peered into Billy's hand at the AA sobriety medallions. He shook his head. "He must've gotten the idea that these women in recovery would make good victims while he was actually attending meetings himself. He wouldn't have attended Ashley's meeting, as that was for women only and there's no evidence yet he attended Tina's, but he obviously attended meetings somewhere."

Billy's hand closed around the medallions. "Who even knows if the guy was in recovery? Could've all been a scam."

"I'm just hoping The Player left as much evidence as Walker when he killed him."

"Don't count on it." Billy held up his fingers and ticked off each one. "No prints at the scene, nobody saw a car, a person, heard a voice, a gunshot, no cameras at the no-tell motel. Looks like a ghost murdered Walker."

"A ghost who used the same weapon that killed the true crime blogger, Sean Hughes, a few months ago."

Billy spread his hands. "Where's the weapon? Where are the prints from Quinn's place? Where are the witnesses from Quinn's place? How are we going to trip up this guy?"

Geoffrey interrupted them, holding a large plastic bag in front of him. "I have some clothes here and a pair of shoes we can test. I think we're going to have some overwhelming evidence against Walker."

"Oh, I forgot." Billy dipped into the pocket of his suit jacket. He held out a prescription pill bottle between his thumb and forefinger. "Here's the pill bottle that belongs to Piper Moss."

"Kyra already contacted Piper to let her know Erica's killer was probably dead. That'll put Piper's mind at ease."

"At least someone's happy about this case." Billy punched Jake's shoulder. "C'mon, man. We've got our guy. He's not going to kill anyone else. He messed up by leaving that witness. It was the beginning of the end for him."

"I'm ecstatic." Jake aimed a finger at his face. "This is my ecstatic look, and you're right. Walker never should've left the witness at the scene and tried to take care of her later."

Knots tightened in Jake's gut. The Player had made the same mistake. Would he fix it twenty years later?

"Don't worry about it. I'm fine." Kyra put her phone on speaker and stuck it in her cup holder. "I'm on my way to the appointment now, and I'm sure Shai will just scratch the surface with me. If I'm too rattled to drive after the session, I'll order a car. You guys killed it today and sealed the deal. I was able to spread good news to all the family members."

"The Player handed him to us. He may have even planted all the evidence so there would be no doubt we had Copycat Four."

"Stop saying that." Kyra squeezed the steering wheel. "Lori lifted Walker's print from Tina's wallet. You would have tracked him down eventually. The Player gave you nothing. He killed Walker out of self-preservation."

"Okay, okay. I'm glad we ended this for the victims—or at least this chapter. It never really ends for them, does it?"

"No. It just becomes a part of you." Kyra blinked. "Hey, I just took the freeway exit for Brentwood. I'll call you when I'm done. Maybe I'll hand you The Player."

"Take it slow and easy... I love you."

Kyra's heart bumped against her chest. Jake usually reserved those words for postcoital bliss, but she'd take them anytime, anywhere. "I love you, too, J-Mac."

She drove the rest of the way to Shai Gellman's office with a silly smile twitching her lips. She parked on San Vicente along the green strip and jogged across the street to the two-story office building with its red-tiled roof and courtyard ringed with fragrant plumeria and jasmine crawling along the low stucco walls. A fountain gurgled in the center of the courtyard, shimmering water tumbling from a lion's gaping jaws. Shai's office occupied the bottom level, tucked beneath the stairs that led to the upper floor.

Leaves floated in little puddles of water left

over from yesterday's rain, encouraged by the shade that shrouded Shai's office door. The gray skies threatened more of the same for this evening, and LA rejoiced at the precipitation that cleared the air and soaked the parched hillsides. Of course, too much saturation could lead to mudslides, and they'd had their share of wildfires at the end of the summer to make that a real possibility. The city always seemed to perch on the cusp of paradise and disaster, sort of mirroring her life.

Shai had a discreet sign by the side of his dark wood door, and Kyra tried the handle. Some therapists locked their front doors to keep all but clients out of their offices. Shai wasn't one of them.

Kyra nudged the door with her hip, and the scent of nag champa engulfed her as she stepped inside the waiting room. A small candle burned in the corner, its flame flickering with the breeze from the open door.

The door to Shai's inner sanctum stood halfway open, and a low voice floated from that room. "Come on in."

Kyra bypassed the button on the wall outside and pushed open the door.

A small-statured man rose from a cushion on the floor and glided forward, a smile wreathing his face. "Welcome. I'm Shai."

Kyra felt his presence like a big, warm hug, and

a smile tugged at her own lips as she extended her hand. "Nice to meet you, Shai. I'm Kyra."

He squeezed her hand between his two soft, chubby ones. "I'm glad you're here. Don't worry. You don't have to sit on the floor—unless you want to. My previous client left an hour ago, and I was meditating."

"I'm sorry I kept you late."

"No apologies, please." He flicked his ponytail, laced with gray, over one shoulder. "This is a blame-free, apology-free zone."

Kyra suppressed a smile. Jake was right about one thing. He would've hated this. Tipping her head toward the door, she asked, "Do you always keep the door to your inner office wide open like that?"

"Only for my last appointment of the day—and you're it." Spreading his hands, Shai said, "Have a seat. Something to drink?"

"No, thank you."

She allowed her own clients to sit where they wanted, although not one of them ever sat in her chair. She would've allowed it and incorporated it into their therapy session. She spotted Shai's place in a second, which had his name written all over it: a comfortable chair, not too deep, with a round table next to it containing a cup of tea and a notebook with a jeweled pen beside it.

She settled in the oversized chair across from his, and immediately felt its comforting embrace.

He sank into his own chair. "Tell me what you know about the memory before we start, Kyra."

"Apparently, I witnessed my mother's murder when I was eight years old. I saw the killer. The detective on the scene wanted to protect me, so he never revealed this to anyone. H-he must've told me when I was a child that I didn't see what I thought I saw. I have no recollection of the event, and I have no recollection of ever thinking I saw the killer. I always believed I'd slept through my mother's murder, and the detective affirmed this over and over throughout my childhood so that it became my truth. It's what I believed until recently when I saw the original police report from that night with the information that I'd seen the killer—and he'd seen me."

Shai steepled his fingers beneath his chin, the expression on his face never flickering. "Did you give a description of the killer in that report?"

"No." She rubbed her hands on her slacks. "Does that sound like an impossible task?"

"The memory exists, whether you can access it or not. It exists. It's never impossible to reach that memory if your mind is open and you truly want it."

"Oh, I want it." She swallowed her last word. Did she? It could mean the identification of The

Player, or it might mean nothing at all. Was she hanging all her expectations on this one memory? What if it didn't have the desired results? She'd have nothing. The prospect of recovering the memory gave her hope. The reality might dash all that hope.

When she met Shai's sparkling eyes, slightly turned up at the corners, she knew he'd read every thought that had crossed her mind.

"Do you want it, Kyra?"

She grabbed the overstuffed arms of the chair and straightened her shoulders. "I do."

"I assume you've been hypnotized before, as you're a therapist yourself." Shai reached over the side of his chair, took a sip of tea and picked up the ornate pen.

"Yes, I've been to a few workshops and underwent hypnosis as part of the sessions." She held up a hand. "Before you ask, yes, I'm susceptible."

"Good." The pen winked in the low light as he waved it at her. "Make yourself comfortable. Release your grip on the chair. I'm going to record our session. Is that all right with you?"

"Fine." Kyra flexed her fingers and then unzipped one of her boots. "Okay to remove my shoes?"

"Whatever works for you." He aimed the pen at a couch. "You can lie down if you like."

"I prefer this chair. I could get lost in this chair. I need one of these in my office."

"Nice, isn't it?" Shai's eyes twinkled. "One of my secret weapons."

Kyra removed her boots and tucked one foot beneath her thigh, relaxing against the cushions. "I'm ready."

Shai held up the gleaming pen. "Another one of my secret weapons. I'd like you to watch it and listen to my voice. Sink into that chair, relax. Unclench every muscle. Clear your mind. Start breathing deeply."

Focusing on the pen that gleamed in the semi-darkness, Kyra pulled in a long breath through her nose and blew it out through her mouth. Something Quinn's wife, Charlotte, used to tell her when she'd run to their house away from another foster home flickered across her brain. In with the butterflies, out with the bees. A smile touched her lips. Were Quinn and Charlotte together now?

Shai's voice soothed her nerve endings. "You're so at ease now, so relaxed. You're warm and comfortable. Your mind is open. Your eyes are starting to get heavy. It's all right. You can close them."

The glow of the jeweled pen got blurry, as Kyra's eyelids fluttered. She'd entered a dark, safe space where Shai's voice guided her.

"You're eight years old, Kyra. You're Marilyn now. Your mother calls you Mimi. You're living with your mother. It's the end of the summer. Hot. Do you remember?"

Her chin dropped to her chest. "Hot. Santa Ana winds. I'm going to start third grade in a week. I like school."

"Good. You live alone with your mother, but there's someone else there that night."

Kyra's eyelids flicked. "That night?"

"The night your mother was murdered."

The darkness became a tunnel, and she was rushing toward a pinhole of light that grew larger and larger as she tumbled through the space. The light blinded her and she squeezed her eyes tight. "Someone killed my mom."

"That's right, Mimi. You were there. You saw him. Do you remember?"

A sharp crack had her scrambling from her bed. Sometimes Mom had friends over—sleepy-eyed men who smiled at her over their morning coffee before they left and she never saw them again. Could Mom be seeing one of those friends tonight?

She crept toward her bedroom door and eased it open. It creaked. Through the crack, she saw Mom on the floor, along with a broken vase—a pretty blue vase that Mom bought cheap at the Salvation Army because the color matched their eyes. Mom always said her eyes would make her a famous actress.

Those eyes now bulged from their sockets as Mom clawed at the gloved hands around her throat. The man on top of Mom had something on his head. A white cap? A stocking?

*Turn around. Turn around.* "Turn around."

The room spun, and Mimi tried to keep her eyes on the man's head. Her vision narrowed, and the tunnel sucked her back into the darkness. "Turn around."

"Kyra?"

Her eyelashes fluttered, and she focused on Shai's face. "I was there. I saw him, but he wouldn't turn around."

"Do you think that's what happened that night? He never did turn around. You never got a look at his face."

She shook her head…hard. "He turned around. I know he did. I expected him to, but I wasn't ready. I wasn't prepared to see him. I noticed he had his head covered with something white or flesh-colored—a cap or maybe a stocking."

"Maybe he pulled a stocking over his face. Maybe that's why your description to the detective was confusing." Shai hunched forward, his forearms on his knees. "How are you feeling? Are you okay?"

"I'm fine." She glanced at Shai's magic pen. "Sh-should we try again?"

He smiled. "Next session."

Kyra stretched her legs in front of her and then pulled on her boots. "Thanks, Shai. I'm confident I can get there."

"So am I. You're a good subject. Most therapists are." He pushed to his feet and tossed his pen onto his desk. "Anything for the road? Water? Coffee?"

"My road's not that long. I'm over in Santa Monica, but thanks." She hitched her purse over her shoulder. "You're staying? I thought I was your last client tonight."

"Just some work to finish up, and I prefer doing it here rather than at home."

Kyra paid for her session, and they scheduled another in two days. She waved at Shai on her way out of the office as he stood by the doorway of his therapy room.

Those clouds from earlier had made good on their promise, and raindrops splattered against the pavers in the courtyard and pinged against the pool of water in the fountain. The heels of her boots clicked as she walked down the sidewalk of the short, empty street that led to the busier San Vicente, where she'd left her car.

As she passed the corner of one building, a slick sound, like someone moving in a wet jacket, caught her attention. The hairs on the back of her neck stood on end, and she reached into her pocket for her pepper spray. Before she could start to pivot on the toes of her boots, an arm came around her from behind and crooked around her throat.

A muted whisper touched her ear. "Now I'm gonna do you like I did your mother."

## Chapter Fourteen

Kyra's muscles coiled and her gaze dropped to the arm in the black jacket that had a stranglehold around her neck. A black glove covered his hand. She tried to twist her head, but the pressure increased. The man's other arm pinned her right arm against her side, and she couldn't get to her purse...or her gun.

But the fingers of her left hand curled around her pepper spray. She wheezed as her attacker squeezed tighter, and she slipped her thumb beneath the release on the canister. In one fluid movement, she pulled her hand from her pocket, aimed the pepper spray over her shoulder and pressed the button.

Immediately, his grip slackened and he hacked. Again, she tried to turn around to get a look at him, but he pushed her hard to the ground. As she hunched on her hands and knees, sucking in air, her assailant stomped on her back and she collapsed.

Still coughing, the muffled sound telling her he had a mask or covering over his face, he kicked her in the side. As she tried to roll over, like a turtle trying to gain purchase, a man's voice rose above the sound of her own harsh breathing.

"Hey, hey. What's going on? Stop!"

Her attacker abandoned his half-hearted efforts to kill her and ran. She felt the whoosh of his jacket as he took off, and she curled into a fetal position.

She needed help. She needed Jake.

JAKE CAREENED ONTO San Vicente and made a beeline for the emergency lights. Kyra had been calm and coherent on the phone, but her voice sounded like that of a three-pack-a-day, thirty-year smoker.

He didn't bother trying to head down the small street off the boulevard, so he parked his car at the corner and jogged toward the two patrol cars and the ambulance. This street contained small office buildings and businesses, not residences, so the crowd of people rubbernecking was smaller than it might have been.

His pace quickened when he saw Kyra sitting in the back of an ambulance, her legs dangling over the back bumper. A small man with a ponytail held her hand.

Jake started talking before he reached them.

"Are you all right? Do you need to go to the hospital?"

She reached out to him with her other hand, a white bandage wrapped around it. "I'm okay."

"You sound…rough. He tried to choke you? What happened to your hand?" He took it gently in his own and traced a finger around the bandage.

"He did choke me. Came at me from behind, and I scraped my hand when I went down." She tried a wink and failed. "But you know me. I never walk alone without a few weapons on me. I got him with my pepper spray."

"Good for you. Did you get a look at him? Did anyone?" He held his breath and glanced at the little man, who smelled like incense.

"I saw his arm as he wrapped it around me— black jacket with a black glove. I could tell from his hold on me that he was about average height, not quite six feet tall. I know he was wearing some kind of mask because his whisper and his cough sounded muted, and I don't think he could've made a renewed attack on me if the pepper spray had hit him full-on in the face."

"Renewed attack?" Jake's pounding heart picked up speed and he turned to the man with the ponytail. "Did you see him?"

"No, I came out later when I heard the commotion."

"Sorry." Kyra drew back into the ambulance so Jake could get a better look at the man. "Jake, this is Dr. Shai Gellman. Shai, this is Detective Jake McAllister."

Jake gripped Shai's pudgy hand but didn't squeeze too hard. "Thanks for coming to her assistance."

"I'm afraid all I did was offer moral support." Shai pointed to a couple talking to an LAPD officer. "They're the ones who stopped the attack."

Jake squinted at the pair. "Did they see anything?"

"Just a man attacking me, but they scared him off." She nudged him. "Go talk to them and the officers. Shai will stay with me, and the EMT is hovering, waiting to prod me with more instruments."

Jake nodded to the EMT on his way to the couple and the patrol officer. He flipped open his wallet to flash his badge. "LAPD Homicide Detective Jake McAllister."

"Homicide?" The woman's gaze darted to Kyra, and she clutched her throat in just about the same area where Kyra's sported angry, mottled flesh. "Isn't she okay?"

"She's fine, but her attack is related to a series of homicides. I know you answered the officer's questions, but did you see the attacker?"

The tall, gangly man jerked his thumb over his

shoulder. "I was picking my wife up from her realty office and walking her to my car that I'd left on San Vicente. There's never enough parking on this street. We saw that woman on the ground by the corner of the building, and a man was standing over her, kicking her."

Hot rage thumped through Jake's veins. "Did you see his face?"

"He was wearing a mask, like a ski mask with slits for his eyes and mouth." The woman covered her face with her hands.

The man continued. "I yelled at him. He didn't even look up. He swung around and took off running. I—I would've followed him, but I didn't know if he had a gun or a knife."

"No, you did the right thing. Did he run toward San Vicente?"

"He ran between those two buildings. That's where I was thinking he was probably hiding. The woman said he surprised her from behind." The guy draped his arm around his wife, who shivered from the rain, or fear. "Did he mug her or something? My wife said I was crazy for picking her up on the nights when she closed out the office by herself because this is a safe area, but you never know, do you?"

"You don't. Keep picking up your wife." Jake clenched his jaw. If he'd been at the appointment with Kyra, this never would've happened.

Jake questioned the couple for several more minutes, and then turned his attention to the officers who arrived on the scene first. They'd canvassed the area and found no other witnesses. Shai only came out when he heard the man yelling at Kyra's assailant. He'd seen nothing.

One of the officers mentioned a camera outside a bank on San Vicente, but as the attacker didn't leave that way, it wouldn't do much good. With a glance at Kyra, still under the ministrations of the EMT, Jake swept aside the fronds of a large sago palm and crept toward the area between the two buildings.

The guy could've easily hidden here, waiting for Kyra, stepped out and secured her around the neck. He could've killed her on the sidewalk, or more likely, could have dragged her back here, out of sight.

He followed the path between the two buildings, which led to a small parking lot. He looked for cameras but found none. The lot abutted the sidewalk of another street. The attacker could've run in several directions.

When he went back to the street where Shai's office was located, the couple had left and the sparse crowd that had gathered had dispersed. The cops had waited for him and promised to send him their report when they had it ready to go.

Jake talked to the EMTs, who were about to

release Kyra, and then he and Kyra walked Shai to his car before turning toward San Vicente together.

When they reached the corner, Kyra grabbed his arm. "You know it was The Player, right? He told me he wanted me dead like my mother. If I hadn't maced him first and that couple hadn't been coming down the street, I'd be dead."

The same thought had been circling in his brain ever since she'd called him to tell him about the attack. He couldn't deny it, and the words he whispered to her proved it. "How did he know you were here? Who knew you were going to see Shai?"

"You, me, Shai and—" her eyes grew big and her body stiffened "—Captain Castillo."

"That's right. You did tell Castillo."

"I—I felt he had a right to know." She pressed a hand against her lower back, where The Player had kicked her, and grimaced. "Captain Castillo is not The Player. If I'd seen my mother's killer and then the same guy waltzed in for the 911 call, I'd have known him then."

"I never thought Castillo was The Player, but how did The Player find out about Shai Gellman?" They'd started walking again, and Jake's legs felt like wooden posts beneath him. Could The Player really be a cop? Who else would Castillo tell, and why?

"I don't know. I swear I only told Castillo." Kyra pulled her keys from her purse and stabbed at the key fob. The lights on her car flashed once.

Jake took in the busy street. Cars whizzed past on either side of the green strip down the middle of the boulevard, and people bustled through the crosswalks to get from their cars to restaurants and from their places of work. "Were you followed?"

"What?" Kyra snapped her head around and winced, grabbing the back of her neck.

"Could someone have followed you from the station? You did come here directly from the Northeast Division without going home first, right?" He eyed her work slacks and sweater beneath her jacket, her hair half in and half out of her customary ponytail she wore for work.

"I did, but I didn't notice anyone following me."

"Did you look?"

"No." She pressed a hand to her forehead. "The Player already knows where I live and work. He doesn't have to follow me, even though I *am* careful when I walk to and from my car. That's why I had the pepper spray ready."

"So, someone could've been following you and you wouldn't have known?" He circled her car as she opened the driver's side door.

"I suppose so." She hunched her shoulders.

"That means he was watching me on the street and knew where I went."

Jake slipped on a pair of latex gloves from his pocket and crouched on the sidewalk next to her car. He aimed the light from his cell phone at her chassis. On his knees, he crawled to the other side of the car, his hand trailing over the metal that comprised the underside of her vehicle. When his gloved fingers stumbled across a rectangular shape that moved when he nudged it, he ducked his head under the car, the light playing over the area where his fingers picked at the device.

He pulled it off and cupped it in his hand as he rose to his feet. "He didn't have to follow you. He attached this GPS device to your car. He may have been on your tail to see where you went when you got here, or maybe he just watched you walk toward the side street and then took up his position."

Kyra seemed to crumple and grabbed on to the car door before she slid to the ground. "How? Where did he do this?"

Jake took two big steps to catch her in his arms. "It's like you said, Kyra. He knows where you live and work. He could've attached it at any time. He even knew your car was parked on the same street as that motel where he told you to find Walker."

"C-can I see it? I want to know what one looks like—just in case." She held out her cupped hand.

"Don't manhandle it on the off chance he left some prints." He held the device out to her, his fingers on the edges.

She took it from him the same way and examined it. "Should I leave it on the car, so I don't tip him off?"

"No." He wiggled his fingers and she placed the GPS in his hand. Using his fingernail, he opened the rectangle and shook out a flat disc. "With the battery gone, it's not going to function."

He snapped the device back together, peeled off one of his gloves and inserted the GPS into the glove, tying it off at the end.

Kyra placed a hand against her throat. "He means business now, doesn't he? No more fooling around. He wants to kill me."

Jake kissed her gently on the lips. "He's gonna have to go through me first."

THE FOLLOWING MORNING, Jake didn't even glance at Kyra's desk when he walked into the task force room. She'd told him she was taking the morning off.

He'd made sure she got home all right last night, put her to bed and hung out in her living room with Spot to keep watch. She had a top-notch security system at her apartment, but there was no way he wanted to leave her after the night she'd had.

Maybe The Player had gotten the jump on her, literally, because she'd been focused on her session with Shai. She confirmed that under Shai's guidance, she'd gone back to the night of her mother's murder and had seen the killer—or at least the back of his head. She'd had a strong sense that The Player had turned around that night and looked at her, but the hypnosis wouldn't take her there—yet.

She'd also been sure The Player had been wearing something over his head or some kind of white or beige cap, which seemed odd—black ski mask like last night, yes, but light-colored cap? Maybe once he turned around, she couldn't see his face, anyway. He didn't like the idea that The Player might know Kyra was seeing a hypnotherapist.

He'd pay a visit to Captain Castillo to make sure he hadn't let that information slip to anyone. As he turned the corner from the war room, he almost plowed into a woman heading the opposite direction and pulled back.

"Sorry."

She brushed her black hair from her eyes and held up her hands. "Totally on me. Mind on other things."

"Guilty." He assessed her athletic frame, and then snapped his fingers. "You're Dina Ferrari, right? I'm Billy Crouch's partner. I know you're helping him with his sister's disappearance."

She thrust out her hand. "Billy may have mentioned you once or twice. Nice to meet you."

"How long have you been in the PI business?"

"Couple of years." She tilted her head, and her straight hair slipped over one shoulder. "Are you vetting me for Cool Breeze?"

"He seems happy with your work." He patted his pocket for the glove with the GPS device tied up inside, and remembered he'd left it at Kyra's place. "I do have a question for you, though, if you don't mind—professional question."

"My favorite kind."

"I thought I read about a program or something you can put on your phone that detects bugs and GPS devices. Do you have something like that?"

"Absolutely. For yourself? The department?"

"Both. I want it on my phone, but it's for work on the task force."

"Tax deductible." She grinned. "I can text you the link and you can buy and download it right to your phone. It's really easy to use, like a scanner. It'll pick up the waves of a bug and the signal of a GPS. You can get a detector that will have your phone emitting beeps and squeals."

"Sounds perfect." He dipped his hand into his

pocket for his personal cell phone and asked for her number. He called her and stored the contact. "Send it to me when you have it. I really appreciate it."

"Anytime, Detective."

Jake continued down the hallway to Castillo's office and listened for voices before tapping on the closed door. At Castillo's invitation, Jake poked his head inside the office.

Castillo's face immediately flushed, and he blinked. Jake was probably the last person Castillo wanted to see.

"Can I have a word?"

"Shut the door." Castillo folded his hands on the desk. "Have you decided what you're going to do yet?"

Jake sat on the arm of the chair. He didn't plan to stay long. "Look, Kyra has the information you and Quinn kept from her all these years, and she's taking steps. I don't see any reason to spread that story around—especially with Quinn's memorial and funeral right around the corner."

Castillo seemed to collapse in his chair. His chin quivered and he wiped a hand across his mouth. "I appreciate that."

Folding his arms, Jake said, "I'm not doing it for you, Castillo. I'm doing it for Quinn and for Kyra. She told you she was seeing a hypnotherapist to recover memories of that night, right?"

"She mentioned it. I told her it was a good idea. She needs to try to remember that night to put it behind her."

"You know The Player attacked her last night."

"Of course I heard. I am still in charge of this task force."

"He attacked her when she was leaving her appointment with the hypnotherapist."

Castillo's sharp intake of breath told Jake he didn't know that part. "Did you mention Kyra's intention to undergo hypnosis to anyone?"

"No." Castillo smacked his hand on his desk. "Why would I do something like that? That only hurts me. You think I blabbed that information, and that's how The Player tracked her down?"

Jake scratched his chin. "No. He had other methods of tracking her down."

Castillo's phone rang the same time Jake's cell buzzed, but instead of dismissing him, Castillo held up a finger. "Hold on."

As the captain answered his call, Jake checked his phone and saw a text from Dina. She worked fast. Jake tapped the link, downloaded the app and paid for it, all while Castillo talked on the phone.

He opened the app and made a few selections, but Castillo interrupted him. "I wanted to let you know that I'm retiring."

Jake glanced up, raising his eyebrows. "You are? You afraid I'm going to rat you out?"

"I just can't be in command of people who don't respect me. You'll never get that respect back for me, and I know it's only a matter of time before you tell Billy. You two tell each other everything, as it should be. You're good as partners and two of the best detectives in the department—and no, I'm not just blowing smoke."

Jake started to answer, but his phone buzzed in his hand and started making chirps and high-pitched squeals. He stared at the red lines jumping on the display and jerked to his feet.

He held the phone in front of him and shifted his gaze to Castillo's wide eyes and open mouth. Jake put his finger to his lips and scribbled on Castillo's whiteboard.

*Your office is bugged.*

# Chapter Fifteen

Kyra sucked in a sharp breath that rasped against her sore throat. She took a sip of tea laced with honey and said, "How do you know Captain Castillo's office is bugged?"

"I ran into Billy's PI at the station, and she sent me a link to a bug tracker that works from phones. I was in Castillo's office playing around with it, and it went off."

Wrapping her hands around the warm mug, Kyra asked, "Did you find the bug?"

"We found it attached to a lamp on his desk—tiny thing. We left it there."

She choked on her next sip of tea, which didn't do her throat any favors. "You left it?"

"We didn't want to tip off anyone listening that we found it. Castillo's leaving the device there and not having any confidential conversations in his office, but we're thinking of a way we can trip up the person who planted the bug."

"What does this mean, Jake?" Kyra massaged

her temples with her fingertips. "Who could possibly get into the captain's office to plant a bug?"

"It could be the cleaning crew." He cleared his throat. "Or a cop."

"You and Quinn always had your suspicions that The Player could be someone on the inside. Nobody wants to think a cop is a killer, working against his coworkers." Kyra picked up the latex glove that contained the GPS tracker from her car and swung it from her fingertips. Was that why The Player always seemed to know where she was? "D-do you think that's how…my attacker knew I'd be at Shai's office last night?"

"Possibly, or it could be the tracker on your car."

"What are you going to do with this information, Jake?"

"Castillo has agreed to keep quiet about it for now. He's going to make a list of people who have been in his office the past few weeks."

"Why two weeks? This could've been going on since the copycat slayings started last summer. He could've been keeping tabs on all the cases."

"Maybe, but bugs have to be replaced at some point."

She swallowed, placing her hand against her bruised neck. "Then what? What are you going to do with Castillo's list?"

He answered abruptly. "Start making discreet inquiries."

"You're going to start investigating members of the task force?"

"I have to, Kyra. Something isn't right when the captain of a task force has his office bugged." Jake paused. "Unless it's Internal Affairs doing the bugging. Maybe they already know Castillo is a dirty cop, and they're trying to catch him in the act. If so, they got an earful the other day when I came to him with what I'd found out about Galecki."

"Can you ask IA without jeopardizing the upper hand you have with this knowledge?"

Jake whistled through his teeth. "I'm not sure. I don't want to play my hand too soon. Let's keep this quiet for now. I'll tell Billy and that's it. We can both do a little investigating on the side— just looking at schedules and possible alibis. We know The Player attacked you last night. We can start looking into the time frame for that, and for the night Walker got whacked."

"I will keep mum."

"How's your throat today? You sound hoarse, like you have a cold."

"It hurts, but it's better than it was this morning. I canceled all my appointments today, and I'm just exchanging emails with the Copycat Killers' victims' families. Tina's and Ashley's friends and families were relieved their killer is dead, and I haven't heard from Erica's family yet." She paused and swirled her tea. "You did find enough evidence in Walker's house and car to tie him to the slayings, right?"

"Oh, yeah. His car was a treasure trove of evidence—hair, fibers, DNA—we got it all. Seems he was only careful when he dumped the body, not when he transported it. He probably figured he'd have time to clean out his car before we got a line on him, but he wasn't counting on his mentor to end his killing spree."

"I'm holding my breath for a fifth. No offense, Detective, but I'm ready for the Copycat Player Task Force to break up."

"I am, too, and I have a feeling we've seen the end of the copycats."

"What makes you say that?" Her muscles tensed. She'd had the same feeling, but the alternative didn't bode well for her.

"The Player ended it himself. He stopped killing after his own reign of terror twenty years ago because he was afraid he'd get caught, or maybe he was locked up during that time, but I think he realizes he's closer than ever to getting nailed today. I think he's done. He can hibernate for another twenty years."

Kyra released a breath. "Except for one loose end."

"He's not going to get to you, Kyra." Jake's phone beeped with a call on the other line. "Stay put today. I'll drop by after work and bring you some chicken soup. Gotta go."

When the call ended, she cupped the phone in her hand and brought up her security cam for the outside of her apartment. Besides her neighbor upstairs and across the way doing his laundry, she didn't see any movement. The Player wouldn't come to her apartment. He must know about the security cameras by now.

He'd never been caught on camera yet—not when he'd run over the homeless woman in Santa Monica after she'd done some dirty work for him, not when he murdered Sean Hughes, the blogger who was in contact with Copycat Three, not when he killed Quinn, not when he shot Copycat Four and not when he attacked her last night. He'd made some bold moves but hadn't shown his hand yet.

Would remembering his face in Shai's office really make a difference? She could help a sketch artist with a composite, but she'd be recalling a man twenty years younger. It could be that her mother knew The Player, and maybe Kyra knew his name, too, as one of her mother's many male *friends*. If that were the case, she could ID him, give him a name, but that's not how The Player operated. He'd killed strangers.

It didn't matter. She'd carry on with the hypnotherapy and hope for the best—even if it were just for her own peace of mind.

She dragged her computer into her lap and rubbed her hands together. More work while she dreamed of chicken soup with Jake.

THE NEXT DAY, Kyra stood in front of the mirror and adjusted a scarf around the bruising on her neck. She didn't need any more attention or sympathy today at the station.

As she gulped down some orange juice standing up in the kitchen, she noticed the glove with the GPS device from her car secured inside on her coffee table. Jake had forgotten to take it with him again. He must be convinced The Player hadn't left prints on it, but Kyra wanted to make sure. She rinsed out her juice glass, stuck it in the dishwasher and swung by the living room to pick up the tracker.

As promised, Jake had delivered the chicken soup last night, along with a box of throat lozenges and probably more tea than had been dumped in Boston Harbor. He'd stayed with her most of the night, but didn't sleep over. He had a busy day today, and she'd shooed him out.

She knew he hated leaving her alone in her own place, but he was also on the feed for her security cams around her apartment. She had a feeling he watched them more obsessively than she did.

An hour later when she got to the station and entered the task force war room, her gaze darted around the desks and studied the faces of the team members. She could usually gauge the point in an investigation by the activity level of the task force. People scurried about today, lots of phone calls and plenty of tapping away on keyboards, but the action lacked the manic, intense feel of when a killer was on the loose. They had their man—or at least one of them.

Her head automatically swung toward Jake's desk, but she knew he'd be out for most of the day. She pulled her laptop from her bag and grabbed the tied-up latex glove, setting it on her desk beside the computer. Once she logged in, checked her messages and sent Shai a text to confirm their appointment later today, she shoved back her chair and grabbed the glove, her phone and her makeup bag to touch up her bruises in the ladies' room.

She waved to Captain Castillo in the hallway on her way to the forensics lab, but had no intention of stepping inside his office as long as the bug was there. He and Jake could figure out a sting on their own. She didn't want someone listening to her.

She swept into the lab, pinching the glove between her fingers. "Ah, Clive. Just the man I was looking for."

He glanced up, the fluorescent light in the ceiling making his bald pate look yellowish. "Hello, Kyra. Can I help you?"

She twitched the scarf at her neck. Those lights would do a number on her bruises, too. The other cops might know about the attack on her the night before last, but not all the techs would know.

Holding out the glove, she said, "Jake found this GPS tracker on my car. He had gloves on when he handled it and dropped it in here. We thought there might be prints."

Clive cocked his head. "Someone's tracking you?"

"Long story."

"This isn't another one of your off-the-record requests, is it, Kyra?" He clenched his jaw.

"No." She placed the glove on the table in front of him, along with her phone and makeup bag. "Jake is fully aware of this and would've brought it in to you himself, but he left it at…in my car, after disabling it, of course. You can call and check with him if you like."

She'd asked Clive to do a favor for her before, and when Jake had found out, he wasn't happy. Clive usually did things by the book.

A smile stretched his thin lips. "I trust you. I

can't get to it right away, though. Plenty of prints to process from Walker's house and car."

"That's fine. Just like the card you dusted for me, I'm pretty certain the person who planted it didn't leave any prints."

"You never know." He untied the glove and withdrew a plastic bag for appropriate evidence labeling. "I'll let J-Mac know if I find anything. Tied to the copycats?"

"Could be." She didn't feel like going into her whole relationship with The Player.

"Hi, Kyra. What brings you to our sweatshop?"

Kyra turned toward the door and smiled at Lori on the threshold. "Are you accusing Clive of being a hard taskmaster?"

"Never. We're just swamped with work right now—that's a good thing."

"And I just dumped some more on Clive, so I'll leave you guys to your work." She twisted back to sweep up her phone and makeup. "Lunch sometime?"

"Absolutely." Lori winked. "Once the chains come off."

Kyra held up her hand to Clive, who'd already bagged and boxed the GPS device. "Thanks, Clive."

Kyra made a detour to the restroom, and when she placed her phone on the vanity, she saw Shai's text message confirming their appointment—the last of the day again.

A few hours later, rubbing the back of her neck, she'd wished she'd suggested lunch with Lori today. Jake's and Billy's desks were still vacant, and it became apparent she had a sandwich from the deli down the block in her future.

She spent the rest of the afternoon tying up some loose ends with the victims' families and discussing Quinn's memorial and funeral arrangements with Terrence. The ME's office had called her this morning and let her know she could have Quinn transported to the mortuary. Terrence had picked one out and told her he'd handle everything, although she'd insisted on meeting him at the funeral home with Quinn's suit.

Jake had texted her a few times and reminded her that he'd be meeting her when her session with Shai ended to follow her home. If he could put a guard on her 24/7, he'd opt for that.

She packed up for the day and tried to tiptoe past Captain Castillo's open office door, but he called out to her. She backpedaled and hung on to the doorjamb. "I was just on my way out."

"I won't keep you. I spoke to Terrence today, and he told me he talked to you about the plans for Quinn."

She nodded. "He knows so much more about

these things than I do, so I'm going to let him take the lead. He's consulting me about a few personal touches, but I sure wish we could catch Quinn's killer before the memorial. It doesn't seem right to hold it when the guy who murdered him is running around."

"Don't lose hope." Castillo winked, and Kyra understood he didn't want to say more.

She didn't, either, and she pulled away from his door with a wave of her hand.

She'd allowed herself an hour and fifteen minutes to get to Shai's office, and turned down San Vicente with ten minutes to spare. Shai's office occupied a street with restricted parking, so that fact relegated her to grabbing a spot along the median strip of San Vicente again. This busy boulevard hadn't given her problems last time, but she balked slightly as she turned the corner onto the street where she'd been attacked.

Her breath flowed a little easier when she saw a few people parking their cars and darting in and out of the office buildings along the tree-lined street. The sun hadn't completely set yet but painted long shadows on the leaf-dappled sidewalk. As Kyra approached the courtyard of Shai's building, she slid her hand into the gun pouch on the outside of her purse—just in case.

She hadn't hit the right mood for a hypnosis today. Taking a deep breath, she approached

Shai's office door and shoved it open. Her greeting died on her lips as she noticed the door to Shai's inner office firmly closed.

He'd told her last time he left that door open for his last appointment—her. The hair on her arms stood on end as a chill rippled up her spine. "Shai?"

She glanced over her shoulder at the courtyard, the trees surrounding it blocking out the setting sun. She slammed the door behind her...and locked it. Pulling her weapon from her purse, she crept toward the door to Shai's inner sanctum and called his name again. As long as she didn't accidentally shoot him, he'd understand her caution.

With the gun gripped in one hand, she tried the door handle with the other. She sucked in a breath as it gave beneath her fingers. Raising her weapon, she pushed open the door, the sweet woodsy scent of the candle barely perceptible over another smell, like wet pennies.

She shuffled into the room. As her eyes adjusted to the low light, she picked out open drawers and papers strewn about the floor. With her heart galloping in her chest, she stumbled toward Shai's desk, her purse sliding from her shoulder, and almost tripped over his legs protruding from behind the desk.

Stifling a scream, she dropped to her knees and grabbed Shai's warm hand. *Warm.* His hand was warm, despite the wound on the side of his head, soaking the carpet with his blood.

He moaned, and Kyra yanked the scarf from her neck and wrapped it around his head. "Hold on, Shai. I'm going to call 911. You're going to be okay."

She sprang to her feet to retrieve her purse where she'd dropped it by the door. As she grabbed it, a clicking sound had her whipping her head toward the outer office and the front door.

Her blood ran cold as she saw the door handle twist.

# Chapter Sixteen

Jake careened around the corner and screeched to a halt behind the emergency vehicles, abandoning his car in the middle of the street. He vaulted over the crime scene tape and grabbed the first officer he saw. "What happened here?"

The cop shook him off. "Sir, you're going to have to wait behind the line."

Jake flipped out his badge with an unsteady hand. "What's going on?"

"Someone was attacked in one of the offices. It doesn't look good."

The wheels of the gurney the EMTs were rolling into the office building courtyard squealed, grating against his ears. Jake swallowed. "I-is she dead?"

"She?" The officer shook his head. "The victim is a male, an older male, and he's still alive."

Relief making his knees weak, Jake staggered through the courtyard, clutching his badge. When he walked into Shai's office, he rushed to Kyra perched on the edge of a chair, and fell to his knees in front of her. Blood smeared her blouse, and dabs of it dotted her cheek.

His hands circled her waist. "Are you all right? What happened?"

A sob bubbled to her lips, and she swayed forward, grabbing his shoulders. "It's Shai. The Player got in here and attacked him."

"The officer out front said he was still alive."

"Barely." Her fingers dug into his jacket. "I thought at first he'd been shot. There was so much blood around his head, but then I saw the paper-weight on the floor later, after the police came. He was here. The Player was here."

"He attacked Shai and then left before you came?" Maybe The Player hadn't known about Kyra's appointment today. He couldn't imagine the killer would give up a chance to harm Kyra.

"He was still here, waiting for me." Her gaze flew to the front door of the office. "When I first walked into the office, I sensed something was off. Shai told me he always left the door to his therapy space open before his last patient. It was open the previous time, but this time it was closed. So when I walked into the office, I closed the door behind me...and locked it."

"You think The Player would've tried to come in behind you?"

Her eyes widened. "I know he did. After I

found Shai, I ran back to get my phone to call 911. Someone was trying the door from the outside. He would've come in, maybe surprised me when I was with Shai."

Jake took her hands in his. "What did you do? Where did he go?"

"I had my gun. I aimed it at the door and told him if he stepped into the office, I'd shoot. Told him if he didn't leave, I'd shoot right through the door. He left."

"You didn't see him?"

"No."

"Did Shai see him?"

"I don't know. Shai was moaning and alive when I found him, but he lost consciousness before the paramedics arrived." Kyra popped up from her chair as the EMTs wheeled the gurney from Shai's therapy room. "Is he going to make it?"

One of the EMTs called out to her. "He's still alive. Still unconscious."

Jake stood up and wandered toward the inner office, where papers littered the floor and drawers and cabinets gaped open. "He was looking for something."

Kyra touched his arm. "I'm pretty sure he was looking for notes from my session two days ago. He wants to know what I'm remembering."

"Then stop remembering." Jake squeezed her hand. "You don't have to remember. We'll catch him this time. We'll stop him. He's stepped back into the light, and he's careless, nervous. He's not the precise killer he was twenty years ago. We'll get him, and you don't have to do another thing."

"No video footage of him, no prints, no witnesses. He's still careful, Jake. He still knows how to play the game. Even if I can give you a description of what he looked like twenty years ago, that might help. It's more than you have now."

A muscled ticked at the corner of Jake's mouth. "Shai's hurt. He's not going to be able to help you anymore. In fact, I'm going to request that Castillo remove you from this task force. You're in communication with all of the victims' families. You work with them, and leave the investigation part to us."

Kyra's eyes flashed blue fire, but then she took a deep breath. "Let's pray Shai is going to pull through."

"I'll call the hospital as soon as they get him there." He touched a finger to her cheek. "You have his blood on you."

"You should've seen my hands before the EMTs cleaned them. I staunched the bleeding on his head wound with my scarf."

"If he lives, it will be because of you."

She dug into her purse for a tissue and dabbed the blood on her face. "I was just going to call you when you came charging in here. You were early."

"As soon as I finished reviewing some evidence with Billy, I took off. Figured I'd park right in front of Shai's office and wait for you in the courtyard. I wasn't going to have you take any chances this time, but I didn't realize he'd come at you another way. I wonder why he didn't just wait for you in Shai's office and ambush you when you came in."

She lifted her shoulders. "He probably didn't know whether or not Shai had any more patients coming. He most likely waited until one left, came into the office, attacked Shai, searched for my session notes and then left before someone else could come. He was probably staking out the courtyard, waiting for me or making sure nobody else was coming."

The hair on the back of Jake's neck stood at attention. "Do you think he knew you had an appointment?"

"I don't know. Maybe he was just here to hurt Shai and search his office. My showing up was the cherry on top."

"Your being alive and unhurt was my cherry." He put his arm around her and pulled her close. "When I saw the emergency vehicles at Shai's office and heard someone had been attacked, everything went dark for me. I thought I'd failed you."

She kissed his jaw. "You never have, and you never will."

BY MIDAFTERNOON THE next day, Kyra knew Jake meant business when he told her he wanted her off the task force and shielded from the investigation into Quinn's murder. He'd given her no updates, and everyone seemed to be tiptoeing around her.

He'd only called to tell her about Shai's condition—holding steady but still not conscious. Jake also believed Shai's hospitalization would put an end to her sessions. But while Jake had slept at her place last night, she'd practiced self-hypnosis and had gotten as far as she had with Shai, stopping in exactly the same place—just when The Player was about to turn and show his face. Maybe without Shai's guidance she wouldn't be able to get any further, but she wasn't going to stop trying.

She didn't think Jake would allow her to ever spend one night on her own again until the task force caught The Player. He'd already invited her over tonight for the entire weekend. It's the only thing that still gave her hope that he'd share the progress of the investigation with her. She didn't think he'd be able to resist talking to her about it all weekend—and she'd be there to encourage him. The weekend couldn't come soon enough.

He and Billy had another busy day with briefings, a press conference and meetings with Chief Sterling. Once the chief found out that Jake and

Billy believed The Player was responsible for Quinn's death, he wanted them to go full speed ahead on the investigation—without her.

She knew Jake and Billy had also started the unsavory task of delving into the whereabouts of some of the cops at the Northwest Division during the times of some of the murders. The cops would also have to be of a certain age and have been around during The Player investigation twenty years ago. She didn't envy them that task, even if the subjects might not ever find out they were under suspicion.

At the end of the day, with most of the task force clearing out, she stretched and ran her hand along her desk. She'd miss this desk, this room, her spot in the corner.

Clive poked his head in the door, peering across the room. "J-Mac and Billy still gone?"

"They left around lunch and I haven't seen them since, and don't think I will." Until tonight, snug in Jake's arms, where she could start to work on him.

She blinked as she noticed Clive still standing there, his brow right up to his shaved head wrinkled. "Can I help you with something?"

His gaze snapped to her eyes, his face smoothing. "Of course. I should be showing you instead."

Her heart bumped in her chest. "Showing me what?"

"It's regarding the GPS tracker found on your car."

She put a hand to her throat, where the bruises from the attack a few nights ago were yellowing. "You found prints?"

"I found...something." He put a finger to his lips and twisted his head to the side, scanning the war room, depleted of most of its soldiers. He lowered his voice. "I know Jake and Billy suspect someone on the inside. I don't want to raise any suspicions or alarms—especially if I'm wrong."

"But if you're right?" Butterflies swirled in her empty stomach, and she flattened her hand against her waist.

"Then I have a pretty good idea who put that device on your car, and that's going to lead us right to The Player."

She grabbed her phone. "I'll text Jake."

Clive inclined his head. "And if I'm wrong? If *we're* wrong? I heard a rumor that J-Mac is kicking you off the task force. Will he allow us to do this little investigation—if he knows about it?"

She stared at the phone in her hand. If she told Jake about this, even if she could reach him now, he'd probably tell her to wait, step back.

Clive continued in a soft voice. "I did a favor for you once, Kyra. Dusted that playing card for prints—off the record. I even caught heat for it.

You said back then you'd buy me lunch. This would be more appreciated than lunch."

"All right. What do you want me to see? Is it in the lab?"

"I need to lift some prints off-site. I can take you over in my car, and we can be back here within an hour. If it's nothing, no harm, and we'll keep it to ourselves. Nobody's reputation takes a hit."

Kyra hesitated. Did Clive mean that he was going to lift prints from a possible suspect on the sly?

His phone rang, and he held up a finger. "My wife. That's right, sweetheart. I am going to be late, but not too late. Dinner is still on with the Carsons. If I have to meet you at the restaurant, I will."

When he ended the call, he held up his phone. "Monthly dinner plans with friends. When I thought I might be taking J-Mac out to this location, I warned my wife, but she's good. Ready?"

If she could hand this to Jake, if she could do this for Quinn, it would make it all worthwhile. "Yes. I need a few minutes to pack up."

"That's perfect. Meet me at my car. It's a white Prius parked on the street." He patted the black bag hanging off one shoulder. "I have my materials."

When Clive left the room, Kyra logged off her

laptop and stuffed it into the case. She grabbed her jacket off the back of the chair and surveyed the room. A few members of the task force talked on the phone or clicked away on their computers. Nobody looked up. If Clive knew Jake planned to boot her off the task force, these team members probably already saw her as persona non grata.

She hitched her bag over her shoulder and strode out of the room to meet Clive. If she and the fingerprint tech could solve this thing, they'd all be singing a different tune—including Jake.

JAKE SAID GOOD-NIGHT to his partner in the parking lot of the station and then made his way to the task force war room. He half expected Kyra to be there, as she hadn't answered his last text, which could mean she was hard at work. He burst through the door and glanced at her empty desk. His gaze shifted to the few task force members still at their desks.

One of the cops called out over his computer. "You just missed her."

Jake smiled to himself. He and Kyra hadn't done a very good job keeping their relationship a secret from the rest of the task force. But he didn't care anymore. She'd be off the task force soon enough. He had to keep her away from the investigation into The Player for her own safety.

She probably hadn't texted him back because

she was driving home to pack some clothes for their weekend—but what he had planned for her this rainy weekend didn't require much clothing.

As he sat at his desk and logged in to his computer, he appreciated the quiet of the room. He and Billy had done some discreet inquiries this morning into the locations of the task force members the past few weeks, and they'd started a spreadsheet listing comparisons between those locations and some pivotal dates in The Player's timeline. He wanted to enter some of that data before he left for the weekend.

Fifteen minutes later, he studied the columns, and data for three task force members jumped out at him. Brandon Nguyen had several absences, but the tech guru was a little young to be The Player. He'd have been about Kyra's age at the time of her mother's murder. Still, he had the computer smarts to connect with the copycats. Detective Ned Verona was the right age and had been friends with Quinn. Quinn would've let Verona into his house without a moment's hesitation. Verona had a lot of absences—due to medical. The guy was getting ready to retire. The third person...

"Detective McAllister?"

He glanced up and realized the room had cleared, except for one cop on the phone and Lori Del Valle, the fingerprint tech, standing at the door. "C'mon in and call me Jake. I'm still working for about another fifteen minutes."

"Just wanted to let you know, all the processing from Detective Quinn's house is complete." She held up her hand, her fingers curled into an okay sign, but she said, "Zero. We didn't get anything of substance, nothing to point to a killer."

"I wasn't really expecting anything, Lori." He waved. "Have a good weekend."

He hunched over his laptop again, but he heard tentative clicks across the floor. When he looked up this time, Lori was planted in front of his desk. "Something else?"

Her cheeks flushed. "I just… I wanted to tell you something, but I don't want you to take it the wrong way."

He shoved his laptop away. He hoped this didn't have to do with his boorish assumption earlier that she didn't have the same level of expertise as Clive. He'd hoped they'd put that behind them. "I'm not going to take it any way. What's on your mind?"

"It's Clive." She held up her hands. "I don't want you to think I'm throwing him under the bus or anything because I want his job. He's supposed to retire anyway."

"Clive?" Jake's pulse ticked up a notch, as he glanced at the third name in the spreadsheet with all the $X$'s in the columns. "What about Clive?"

Lori blew out a breath. "He's been doing some weird things with the evidence on these copycat cases, and even Detective Quinn's crime scene."

A rash of tingles spread across the back of his neck. "What kind of weird things?"

"Well, for one, there was a glass from Quinn's place, and Billy asked us particularly to process it for prints."

"And? From what I understood, there were no prints on the glass."

"That's what Clive put in the report, but that's not altogether true. He never dusted that glass for prints."

Jake's fingertips were buzzing now. "Did you question him about it?"

"I—I didn't." Lori twisted her fingers in front of her. "I wanted to, but that was just after I discovered Walker's prints on Tina's wallet. Clive put me on his blacklist for that."

"For discovering the prints of a killer on a victim's wallet?"

"He told me I shouldn't have done it in the field. I should've brought it back here and let him do it."

"Why would he be upset? It all worked out."

"Did it all work out for him?" She squared her shoulders. "This is what I almost told you at the scene of Tina's car that day. He's been playing fast and loose with these fingerprints. I think he's destroying evidence."

There it was. Lori's words punched him in the gut.

"There's something else. He bagged a GPS device the other day in the lab, but when I looked for a record of it later, I couldn't find it. He never logged it."

"GPS device?" Jake could barely hear his own voice over the roaring in his ears. He'd left the box at Kyra's. "Where'd he get it?"

"Kyra dropped it off for him."

Jake had pushed back from his desk and was out of his chair before he even knew he was standing. He called to the cop on the phone. "Holt, Holt."

Officer Holt jerked his head up and put the phone down. "Yes, sir?"

"You said I just missed Kyra. Did you see her when she left? Did she leave alone?"

"Yeah, she did. She left by herself—after she talked to someone, all hush-hush."

Jake's tongue felt thick in his mouth. "Who was she talking to?"

"The fingerprint guy—Clive Stewart."

Fifteen minutes later, Jake turned down Clive's street in Studio City. On his way out of the station's parking lot, he noticed Kyra's car, which he hadn't seen when Billy dropped him off. Had she actually gone with Clive in his car? To his home? Why would she do that?

His hands gripped the steering wheel. Why not? She knew Clive. Clive had done a favor for her in the past. Had he lured her with the GPS?

He'd called a patrol car on his way, and one sat across the street from Clive's house now. He'd break down the door himself if he had to get Kyra out of there.

He knew Clive was married. Was his wife out of town? A dark blue compact sat in the driveway of the tidy house. He thought he'd seen Clive get into a white Prius at the station.

The officers got out of their car, and Jake held up his hand. If Clive had Kyra in this house, he didn't want to spook him.

He stepped onto the porch and rang the doorbell. Maybe Clive hadn't tried anything yet, and Jake could just walk Kyra out of there with the pretense that he had important news for her and knew she had left with Clive. His thoughts stumbled to a stop when a middle-aged woman with blond, chin-length hair opened the door, her eyebrows arched into question marks.

"I'm Detective Jake McAllister. Is your husband at home?"

"My husband?" She drew her sweater around her body in a protective gesture.

Jake showed her his badge. "Clive. I, uh, work with him at the department."

"That bald-headed piece of..." Her hoarse laugh ended in a smoker's cough. "He's not my husband."

Jake stuffed his badge back into his pocket. "You're not Mrs. Stewart? Isn't this Clive's house?"

"Technically, it's still his house, still in his name, but we're divorced. Have been for years. The guy's a creep with mommy issues." She shrugged her shoulders and narrowed her eyes. "This isn't a work call, is it? Did he finally snap?"

Although he was sure the ex-Mrs. Stewart could tell him stories about Clive to curl his hair, he didn't have time to listen. "Where is he? Where does he live now?"

"He lives somewhere in Hollywood. I can't give you the exact address because I don't know it."

Jake slumped. How would he find him? They'd have to ping his phone, Kyra's phone. That could take hours when he probably had minutes. "Do you have anything that might have his address on it? Old mail? Paperwork?"

"No, and he moved recently."

"He moved to Hollywood or he was living in Hollywood and moved?" He'd have to wrap up this conversation that was going nowhere for a chance to ping those phones.

"He moved *to* Hollywood, and no, I didn't ask and he didn't tell me. A friend told me."

"Does this friend have his address?"

"No."

"All right. Thanks, Mrs…" He turned away and waved off the cops.

As he headed toward the sidewalk, his phone already in his hand, Mrs. Stewart called after him. "My friend doesn't have the exact address, but she did see him walking into a fancy high-rise in Hollywood. You know, that one that has a view of the Hollywood Hills, if you're on the right side. I wondered how the hell he afforded that. You know the one I mean?"

Jake knew exactly which one she meant. The plate glass window in his house looked out onto it every night.

# Chapter Seventeen

Kyra blinked as Clive pulled into a subterranean garage off of Sunset Boulevard. The darkness was a sharp contrast to the bright lights of the boulevard, where the neon of the flashing signs did battle with the headlights and taillights streaming below them. Those lights had blurred before her eyes, and she swallowed against her dry throat.

She'd thought her throat was improving, but it felt like sandpaper now, and she grabbed the bottle in the cup holder, downing another few sips of the water Clive had offered her when she climbed into his silent electric car. The action of tipping her head back caused the dizziness she'd felt earlier to come crashing down on her in waves. She put her fingers to her temples.

"Are you all right?"

"I feel a little…strange. Is this where we're going? This building?"

"Yes, someone from the station lives here,

someone who's been showing too much interest in the fingerprints we've been processing from Quinn's house." He reached into the back seat and patted his black bag. "I'm going to lift some prints, and then we're going to compare them against what I found on the GPS that was attached to your car. If they don't match, no harm, no foul, right?"

"Right." She rubbed her head. "Who lives here?"

"I don't want to say just yet." He parked the car in a slot, and she peered at the number painted on the wall in front of them.

She read the numbers aloud. "2021. Are you parking in someone's space?"

"Don't worry about it. I've scoped out this place already. I know what I'm doing."

Kyra shook her head. What were they doing here? Fingerprints. Fingers. All those missing fingers. Her mother's missing finger.

Clive patted her shoulder. "Are you up for this, Kyra? If you're not feeling well, I can leave you in the car. I just thought you'd want to be a part of this…after all you've been through."

"I do. I do." All those missing fingers.

Clive grabbed his bag and slipped out the driver's side door.

Kyra grabbed the door handle on her side but continued to sit. She wasn't afraid, just…tired.

Clive opened the door for her and helped her

out, as if she were ancient, older than Quinn. She stumbled, and he steadied her.

"It's all right. At least we don't have to walk up all those stairs."

He chuckled, and the sound made her feel nauseous for some reason. She'd never heard Clive laugh before. In fact, she'd never heard Clive speak so many words before in all the time she'd known him. And she'd known him…twenty, no, two years. Two years.

He held her arm as he steered her to the back of the parking garage, away from the glass doors.

She pulled against him. "Shouldn't we go that way?"

His grip on her arm tightened, his strong fingers digging into the flesh of her arm beneath her jacket. "I told you. I did reconnaissance first. If we go up the back way and use the freight elevator, nobody will see us. I'm good at reconnaissance."

He marched her silently to a large, dark elevator that smelled like oil. The doors squealed as they opened and shut, and it lumbered up and up. Nineteen, twenty. When it settled, he steered her out of the car, pushed open a fire door and led her to a solid door. When he pulled out a key, she twisted away from him. But when he opened the door, he shoved her inside.

The fog in her brain parted for a few seconds

and she grasped at the truth, but it slithered away from her, and she stood in the middle of the sparsely furnished room with her head tilted to one side. "Who lives here? Why are we here?"

Clive clicked his tongue. "I'll tell you later, and we'll gather the prints and run to McAllister with our proof. You'd like that, wouldn't you?"

She nodded, dropping her chin to her chest. She'd tell Jake tonight as he cooked dinner for them—steaks and red wine again.

"But first I want to show you something."

His voice startled her, and she lifted up her head with a Herculean effort, noticing for the first time the telescope positioned at a large window that looked out on the lights of Hollywood—and the hills beyond.

Clive hunched over the telescope, and the recessed lighting in the ceiling glowed on his bald dome, creating a white circle like a cap on his head. *Turn around. Turn around.* The words found their way to her lips. "Turn around."

Clive turned his head, and Kyra was staring into the dark eyes of her mother's killer...again.

"Oh, I see you finally figured it out, little Mimi. Kyra's a big improvement over Mimi and for sure a big improvement over Marilyn Monroe Lake. Who the hell names their kid Marilyn Monroe? But then, your mother, Jennifer, was a dumb bitch. And a whore. Like my mother. Like my ex-wife. Like you."

She reached for her purse with her gun and realized she'd left it in the car—along with the drugged water.

Instead, Clive pulled out his own weapon and crooked his finger. "Come here. I want to show you something."

Kyra peeled her feet from the carpet and lumbered toward him. Could she push him through the glass? Wrestle the gun away from him? Throw something through the window to attract attention?

Stepping aside, he tapped the telescope. "Have a look. I think you might be interested in what I can see from up here."

She approached the telescope as he adjusted it for her height. When she put her eye to the eyepiece, the view took in the Hollywood Hills across Sunset Boulevard, and as Clive turned a knob on the lens, Jake's house came into focus.

She gasped and staggered back, sinking to the floor, the phone in her jacket pocket digging into her hip.

Clive chuckled, causing her to heave. He'd chuckled the night he turned around and met her eyes after murdering her mother. "Do you know how I know you're a whore, Kyra? I've seen you—all of you. I've watched as *J-Mac* took you against that window, in full view of everyone, your naked body pushed up against the glass. That's how much he cares about you. He knows you're a whore, too."

She couldn't dwell on that right now, couldn't think of Jake, who had no idea where she was. She might be able to watch him from here, pacing his living room floor, calling her, wondering where she'd gone. Wondering if she'd given up on him after he told her he was taking her off the task force. The old Kyra would've done that. But she wasn't the old Kyra. She was the Kyra Quinn always deserved. The Kyra Jake deserved.

She cleared her throat. "You killed Quinn."

"I did." He almost sounded disappointed in himself. "I always liked Quinn, but he was a loose end. His obsession with you is what got him killed. Same with your foster brother, Matt. That's how I was able to keep track of you all those years—first through Quinn and then through Matt."

She had to keep him talking, keep herself active. If she curled up in a corner, she'd die here. The drugs had made her stupid, fuzzy, slow, but she could fight against their effects.

"Why did you stop killing twenty years ago?" Kyra struggled to her feet, stuffing her hand in her pocket and tracing the phone with her fingers.

Clive probably thought the phone was still in her purse, along with her gun.

"Technology and new advancements in law enforcement." He flicked his finger against the telescope, where it pinged. "Improvements in DNA testing, mitochondrial DNA testing, genetic databases with idiots sending their DNA in to trace ancestors, cameras everywhere, cell phones, GPS tracking. It's tough being a serial killer today."

"You'll excuse me if I save my pity for the victims."

Clive's lips stretched into a smile. "I admire your...tenacity, Kyra. There were plenty of forces to beat you down, but they never defeated you—until now. I suppose you have Quinn to thank for that. He rescued you, didn't he? He and Charlotte."

"He let you into his house?" She smoothed her thumb across the face of her phone, feeling the imprint of the home button. She had voice activation on her phone and could call or text Jake, but what could she say in the few seconds allotted before Clive stopped her? Maybe just a simple *I love you*.

"Of course. Quinn knew me from the old days. Just like Jake and Billy, Quinn never suspected me. Oh, he may have suspected a cop or two or someone on the inside, but not me." He spread his hands, and for the first time, Kyra noticed their wiry strength. "He let me in, and I avoided witnesses and cameras like I always do. Told him I had something I wanted him to look at regarding The Player case, *my* case. He got us water. I followed him back to the living room and whacked him on the side of the head to make him go down. Then I shot him up with a stimulant. I guess something about how I replaced his shoe and sock tripped me up."

"Something else tripped you up." Kyra placed her thumb on her phone's home button. She had to wander away from him to give herself more time on the phone. "You left your prints on that glass, didn't you?"

His dark eyes narrowed. "How do you know about that? Did that nosy Lori Del Valle tell you something?"

A pulse throbbed in her throat. Did Lori suspect something about Clive? "Lori told me nothing about you. I figured it out myself when I was at Quinn's place. What happened to that glass?"

"I bagged it for processing, but alas—" he threw up his hands "—there were no prints on it."

"I'm sure you saw to that, just like all the other prints in this case. What happened with Fisher's print on the tape? How did that one slip through?"

The nostrils of his long, thin nose flared. "J-Mac found it at the crime scene. It was a patent print the idiot left. J-Mac saw the print with his bare eyes. I had to process it."

"You killed Yolanda, the homeless lady who helped you send those emails to me and Sean Hughes, the blogger who was communicating with Copycat Three."

"Yes, yes." He waved his hand with the gun in the air. "I took care of all of them, and no, those were not satisfying kills. I did those out of necessity."

"What makes it satisfying for you? What made Clive Stewart a serial killer? Don't you all blame it on your mothers? You called your mother a whore. Is that why other women deserve to die?" She licked her lips. The adrenaline from the knowledge that she finally faced The Player had counteracted the drug in her system, but she still wasn't ready to fight...and he had the gun. She knew he didn't want to shoot her. He wanted to strangle her...just like he did her mother.

"It's a boring tale."

"I doubt that. Why the playing cards? Why the severed fingers? If you're going to kill me, I think I deserve to know. We've been at this game for twenty years, you and I. Before it ends for me, I'd like to know the rules." She meandered toward the window and gazed at the lights below. Too far to jump.

Clive chuckled again and moved toward the

door, the gun still clutched in his hand, as if he feared she'd make a run for it now that she'd recovered her faculties. Could she?

"I guess you have a point there, Kyra. I do feel…close to you. You were the only one alive who knew who I was, who I really was, even though you couldn't remember."

"Who was your mother?"

His gaze locked on to her face from across the room, his own a pale oval against the door. "She was a blackjack dealer in Vegas, part-time hooker. Kind of like your mother."

Kyra nodded in encouragement. She'd always known her mother had traded certain favors for money. Had Clive targeted women like that? Not quite prostitutes but working on the fringes of the sex trade—independent contractors?

"You know what they called her, Mimi?"

"What did they call her, Clive?"

"Pinky." He held up his hand and wiggled his little finger, the one he'd severed from all his victims. "She'd worked in a cannery when she was a teenager and lost her finger. It didn't stop her from dealing, and they all called her Pinky."

The playing cards, the trophy finger—all formed from his messed-up childhood. Her foster brother, Matt, had been abused as a child, shuffled around in foster homes, and had wound up a junkie, in and out of jail. Her own childhood had gone horribly off the rails, and if it hadn't been for Quinn and Charlotte, she could've ended up like Matt. But they hadn't launched a career as a killer.

"Wh-where are all the fingers? You had the copycats take the fingers for you. Did it give you the same thrill?"

"Sadly, it didn't, and now I'm bored with all this. I have one more kill on my list, and then I'm going to retire. I'm retiring from the LAPD, and I'm retiring from killing."

"No, you won't."

His head jerked up. "Excuse me?"

"You won't give it up. You can't. You're driven, and eventually you'll get caught. You don't even seek the fame, do you? You get satisfaction from the perfection of the crime, but you had an unfair advantage. You're not that special, Clive. Once you're no longer *the* fingerprint guy, others will be able to track you down."

"Shut up. I'm tired of hearing you talk. You should be almost comatose by now, but no. You just keep going and going." His face sported red flags and his cheeks puffed out as if he were ready to explode.

She had to make a move. In a loud voice, she said, "I should text Jake."

She shouted the last two words as she pressed her home button and dragged her pocket close to her face. The phone responded in an automated voice, "What do you want to say?"

Clive sputtered and launched forward, shouting something unintelligible.

She brought the phone from her pocket and said the first thing that came to her head. "Twenty, twenty-one, building off..."

Clive tackled her, and they both hit the window hard, the phone flipping out of her hand and spinning across the floor. He smacked her hard across the face, and she kneed him in the groin.

Grunting, he staggered back, but kept the gun pointed in her direction. If he squeezed off a shot, he'd hit her somewhere.

She kicked the telescope, and it topped over on him. She dropped to the ground as he fired the gun. The ear-splitting noise buffeted her eardrums. The window beside him cracked, spider webs rippling along the glass.

She crawled toward his legs beneath a table. If she could wrap her arms around them, she could push him toward the damaged window. They might both go over and fall twenty floors—one for each year of their acquaintance—but she'd put an end to The Player.

Clive steadied himself, bracing one hand against the shattered glass and spotting her under the table. He swung the gun downward.

Kyra coiled her muscles, getting ready to

spring, when a loud commotion came through the front door.

Miraculously, Jake's voice bellowed across the room. "Drop it, Clive."

Clive took a step toward Jake, but he wanted her more. He aimed the gun at her between the table legs. She heaved up, lifting the table on her back, ready to rush him.

Another shot rang out, and Clive's eyes widened. He squeezed the trigger of his gun, and the bullet splintered the wood next to her face.

A volley of three, four shots blasted from across the room, and Clive's body danced with the bullets, the window cracking behind him even more. With the gun still in his hand, he staggered back and fell through the window—twenty floors to his certain death.

# Epilogue

"I don't get it, Daddy. How'd you know where The Player was holding Kyra? She only gave you the apartment number." Fiona tucked a leg beneath her on the couch and pulled a pillow into her lap.

Jake crossed the room to the plate glass window overlooking the city, the lights even more brilliant in Christmas finery, and crooked his finger at his daughter. "Come here."

She handed the pillow to Kyra seated next to her on the couch and skipped to her father.

Slinging one arm across her shoulders, he pointed out the window, his finger smudging the glass. "You see that building across the way?"

"The tallest one with all the windows?"

"That was the building."

Fiona's mouth dropped open, and she twisted her head to look at Kyra. "For reals? But how'd you know it was that one?"

"I thought Clive was still married and living

in Studio City. We all did. But when I got to his house, his ex-wife told me her friend had seen him recently walking into a high-rise on Sunset. I knew right away it had to be that building."

Kyra called from the couch, just to remind Jake. "I always felt something creepy about that window being exposed to the world."

Fiona turned wide eyes back to the view. "So you went straight to that building from The Player's house?"

"I did, and called backup on the way, but when I got there, I didn't know where to go or where to look. I got the building manager to let me look through the tenants, but Clive didn't live there under his own identity. I was ready to search floor by floor, unit by unit, pull a fire alarm, bring the whole building down if I had to. Then I got Kyra's text. I knew the building had over twenty floors, so I had the manager check the tenant for 2021, and who do you think I found?"

Fiona breathed out with awe of her father. "Clive Stewart? No, wait, The Player?"

Jake tapped on the glass. "Jack Spade."

"Jack Spade, like in the jack of spades card?"

"That's right. When I saw that, I knew. The manager gave me the key. I came up with a SWAT team and listened at the door for a few seconds. When I heard the gunshot, I barreled into the room and uh…stopped him."

Fiona nodded and flicked back her ombré-tinted hair. "You shot him and he fell through the window."

"He had a gun in his hand. He was threatening Kyra."

"Oh, I know you wouldn't have shot him unless you had to, but it's still badass."

Jake cleared his throat. "It's late. If you're going to spend the weekend at Lyric's, you'd better get to bed."

"Mrs. Becker promised to keep an eye on us all weekend, so I won't get kidnapped again."

Jake pulled his daughter close and kissed the side of her head. "I have it all worked out with Mrs. Becker."

"Thanks, Dad." Fiona kissed her father on the cheek and sauntered back to the couch, where she leaned over and hugged Kyra from behind. "I'm so glad you're okay, Kyra. Were you scared when you figured out Clive was The Player?"

Kyra brushed the girl's smooth skin with her fingers. "Remember how scared you were when your cute internet boyfriend turned out to be Copycat Three and kidnapped you?"

"Don't remind me."

"I was that scared."

Fiona dropped a kiss on top of Kyra's head, which made Kyra's heart melt. "I'm glad you're safe, and I'm glad you're gonna marry Dad and be my stepmom."

"Me, too." Kyra squeezed Fiona's hands.

Fiona stepped back and ran up the stairs. She stopped midway, clutching the banister, looking down at them shyly through her lowered lashes. "Are you guys gonna give me some siblings? Mom and Brock refuse. Brock has his two kids from his first marriage, and Mom has me, and that's it for them."

Laughing at Jake's stuttering, Kyra stood up and stretched. "I think we can manage that. Now, go to bed before you give your father a heart attack."

When Fiona traipsed up the stairs with a flourish, Kyra joined Jake at the window. "You really should get some drapes."

"That would ruin the whole dramatic effect." He curled an arm around her waist. "Are you going to start making changes when you move in here?"

"You still have time for your bachelor life before the wedding, and I still need to do some work on the Venice house before I rent it out."

"Quinn's memorial was fitting, wasn't it? Was it everything you wanted?"

"And more. Terrence did a spectacular job."

"And you. Your touches made it special."

"In the end, Quinn did help catch The Player.

If Clive hadn't left his prints on that glass at his house and Lori hadn't noticed the irregularities in Clive's behavior, you never would've suspected Clive."

"And if Quinn hadn't raised you to be the... badass you are, I never would've found you." He rubbed a circle on her back. "Do you really want to finish your sessions with Shai?"

"As soon as he's a hundred percent. I owe it to my mom to remember, really remember those last moments of her life. I'm not afraid."

"I know you're not. That's one of the many things I love about you. You're fearless in everything you do."

"Not so fearless in love." She cupped his strong jaw in her hand. "Not until I met you."

He bent his head to press his lips against hers, and his kiss scorched her, took possession of her very soul. He murmured against her mouth. "I suppose making love against this window is out now."

"Um, yeah, especially with your daughter upstairs." She flattened her hands against his chest. "Besides, you have a perfectly good bed with just about the same view, minus the potential for peepers. I think that will work just as well to get going on Fiona's request."

"Let me put a ring on it first." He swept her up in his arms and carried her to the staircase.

"But I'm not opposed to giving you a preview of things to come."

As he held her in his arms going up the stairs, she dropped her head to his shoulder and took in the view of the city lights. From here, the beauty outweighed the evil. Somewhere out there were young women just like her mother, with hopes and dreams. People cared. They helped each other heal and recover. They struggled. They trusted each other. They fell in love.

LA *was* the city of angels, and she'd finally found hers.

\* \* \* \* \*

*Don't miss the previous titles in*
*A Kyra and Jake Investigation series:*

The Setup
The Decoy
The Bait

*Available now wherever*
*Harlequin Intrigue books are sold!*

# Get 4 FREE REWARDS!

## We'll send you 2 FREE Books
## plus 2 FREE Mystery Gifts.

**Harlequin Romantic Suspense** books are heart-racing page-turners with unexpected plot twists and irresistible chemistry that will keep you guessing to the very end.

FREE Value Over $20

M

# WILLARD'S
## *Magnificent*
# MOVIE
# TRIVIA